Conscious that she was soaking wet, Cassidy walked softly into the apartment and called her boss's name.

When she didn't get an answer she glanced out the windows, momentarily mesmerized by the sunset, and nearly dropped the jacket-wrapped parcel when Logan prowled up behind her.

Cassidy gasped at the sight of him sweat soaked in a singlet top that did little to disguise his ripped chest and washboard abs, and tiny gym shorts that hugged his powerful thighs. He had earbuds in his ears and she could hear the pounding music from where she stood.

For a moment she couldn't speak, her body frozen from the impact of all those bronzed, pumped-up muscles glistening with sweat and vitality.

He swiped the towel across his face and through his hair.

"What are you doing here? And why are you dripping all over the floor?"

With two university degrees and a variety of false career starts under her belt, **Michelle Conder** decided to satisfy her lifelong desire to write and finally found her dream job. She currently lives in Melbourne, Australia, with one superindulgent husband, three self-indulgent (but exquisite) children, a menagerie of overindulged pets and the intention of doing some form of exercise daily. She loves to hear from her readers at michelleconder.com.

Books by Michelle Conder

Harlequin Presents

Duty at What Cost?
The Most Expensive Lie of All
Hidden in the Sheikh's Harem
Defying the Billionaire's Command
The Italian's Virgin Acquisition
The Billionaire's Virgin Temptation
Their Royal Wedding Bargain

Conveniently Wed!

Bound to Her Desert Captor

One Night With Consequences

Prince Nadir's Secret Heir

The Chatsfield

Russian's Ruthless Demand

Visit the Author Profile page at Harlequin.com for more titles.

Michelle Conder

CROWNING HIS UNLIKELY PRINCESS

HARLEQUIN
PRESENTS

Recycling programs
for this product may
not exist in your area.

ISBN-13: 978-1-335-14854-4

Crowning His Unlikely Princess

Copyright © 2020 by Michelle Conder

This edition published by arrangement with Harlequin Books S.A.

For questions and comments about the quality of this book,
please contact us at CustomerService@Harlequin.com.

Harlequin Enterprises ULC
22 Adelaide St. West, 40th Floor
Toronto, Ontario M5H 4E3, Canada
www.Harlequin.com

Printed in U.S.A.

CROWNING HIS UNLIKELY PRINCESS

To Heather, the international twin, for so many years of love, friendship and laughter. And all the times you stopped outside a bar to see who was inside!

And to Charlotte, my editor: without you this book would not be half as good.

CHAPTER ONE

CASSIDY CHECKED THE prospectus in her hand against the one on her computer screen and felt her stomach sink to her toes.

She had given him the wrong one.

She was doomed.

She would be fired.

This was it.

After a day that had started out badly and only got worse as it had progressed, it would be the tip of the iceberg.

She hadn't had a day as bad as this one since her father had moved her and her sister out of the small parish in which they had grown up during the middle of the night all those years ago as if they had been criminals. They hadn't been, but for a while they had been treated like they were. And she'd contributed to that, hadn't she?

But beating herself up about past mistakes wasn't going to help her now.

If she didn't fix this, her meticulous boss would be heading to an important meeting in Boston the fol-

lowing morning to finalise the capital investment they
needed for a major project with the wrong information.
That would be eight months of painstaking work down
the tubes. After the unexpected bombshell her sister
had dropped on her this morning that had set off her
day from hell, it was the last straw.

And she had no one to blame but herself. She should
not have let Peta's unexpected news derail her as much
as it had, and she could either sit here and feel sorry
for herself or she could get on and fix it.

And she still had time, she noted, checking her
watch.

She double-checked the updated version of the doc-
ument, ensuring that the right figures were in the right
place this time, and hit the print button.

Of course the printer ran out of paper halfway
through but that was to be expected. It should be one
of Murphy's laws that when a day started out badly
you should just go back to bed and pull the sheet over
your head.

Her forehead throbbed as she recalled how she had
barely been awake when one of her eleven-year-old
twin nieces had come careening into her bedroom
with the news that their mother was getting married.
Her mother, and Cassidy's sister. The one who had
moved in with her after she had hit rock bottom again.
The one who had sworn off men after she'd become a
teenage mother and been dumped by the twins' father
before they had even been born.

Peta had come into her room after that with a sheep-
ish grin on her face and a diamond ring on her finger.

'I wasn't sure how to tell you,' she'd said, half grimacing, half smiling. 'Dan completely surprised me with his proposal and he wants me and the girls to move in with him right away. Not that we will,' Peta had rushed to assure her. 'Not until you find another place to live, or a flatmate, because I know you can't afford the rent here on your own.'

Shell-shocked, Cassidy had just looked at her. 'You're engaged?'

'I know, right?' Peta had stared down at her ring with a stunned but delighted expression. 'I can't believe it either but… He's so special, Cass. And he even wants to adopt the twins.'

A lump had formed in Cassidy's throat at that. The twins were hers! She had been at their birth, she had helped her sister raise them, she had taken Amber to the emergency department when she'd broken her arm and Peta had been stuck on the other side of the city at work. She had been the one to read stories to April to take her mind off her twin in the operating room while they'd waited.

Dan was… Dan was… He was a nice guy, a lovely guy, but marriage?

In hindsight she should have been more prepared for it. Her sister was one of those uniquely beautiful people that made others do a double-take.

Like her boss. Prince Logan of Arrantino.

They moved through life on another level from the more ordinary folk like herself, turning heads and breaking hearts as they went.

It had always been that way. Growing up, the boys at

high school had only ever shown an interest in Cassidy to get an introduction to her sister. It was something she had grown so used to that even now she always questioned a man's hidden agenda before accepting an invitation to dinner. Not that she'd had many of those since the last guy she'd dated, who had only wanted her for her study notes. After the disastrous incident in high school, which she refused to think about, she really should have known better.

Just once she'd like to meet a man who wanted her for her body. Was that too much to ask?

An image of her boss leapt into her head and she immediately banished it. The only reason he would ever want her body was to bury it after he murdered her for making so many errors today.

First by putting through a phone call from a teary ex, hoping for a second chance, instead of the CEO of their law firm, and then for mixing up the restaurant where he was supposed to meet a client for lunch. She'd confused the luncheon date with one he was scheduled to have the following day and he'd been twenty minutes late as a result.

Now this debacle... She stacked the copies of the prospectus carefully on the table. The last thing she needed to do was to drop them as she raced down the stairs to the copy room and set about binding each one into a shiny booklet.

At this time of the evening the office was basically empty, most of her work colleagues at the bank having already gone home, so she was alone with her self-recriminations.

Which she was eternally thankful for.

The thought of having to make polite small talk with a colleague, or returning home before she could paste on her face a genuinely happy smile for her sister, was too much right now. Not that she wasn't genuinely happy for her sister. She was. She was just afraid of what it meant for her.

Afraid to face a future without seeing her family on a daily basis. Afraid to face a future with no one special in her life ever. She could almost see herself now, an unmarried woman with a shawl around her shoulders to keep out the chill, and a dozen feral cats fighting over bowls of cat food.

Her throat thickened. She and her sister were a team. They had been ever since the twins had been born when Peta had only just turned seventeen, and Cassidy eighteen. With their mother having walked out two years earlier, and their father struggling to keep his head above water, Cassidy had become the rock everyone leaned on. Which had been fine with her. She liked helping out, and she had never been the kind of person who walked away when the going got tough.

Glad that she kept up her fitness routine, she took the stairs two at a time as she returned to her office and dropped the glossy prospectuses on her desk, automatically reaching for her phone to dial the courier service.

Then she hesitated.

It would be her luck that the courier either didn't show up or had an accident and the prospectuses ended up at the bottom of the Hudson. Not only would that be an environmental hazard, it would mean she could still be sacked for stupidity.

Being hired as Logan's EA a few months out of college two years ago had been an amazing coup and she'd pinched herself for months afterwards at having landed such a lucrative role.

She knew she had only got it because she had been in the right place at the right time and the HR manager had been desperate. Otherwise she wouldn't be where she was today. Working in a job that she loved for a man who was called a business genius by anyone who mattered. He was a commanding force who stopped at nothing to get what he wanted. Which had intimidated the heck out of her when she'd first come to work for him, but which she'd been advised not to show.

'His previous EAs left because they either couldn't keep up with the demanding workload,' the fastidious HR manager had informed her as they'd marched down the hallway for her interview with her boss, 'they were intimidated by the fact that he's a prince and second in line to the throne of Arrantino, or they fell in love with him. Any of these three will have you out the door in seconds.'

Down to the last few dollars in her bank account Cassidy had assured the immaculately groomed manager that love was so far off her radar it didn't even register as a blip. On top of that she'd held down two jobs and still come out top of her class during her senior year at high school so she knew nothing else other than hard work.

Cassidy stared at the ten prospectuses she'd just

wrapped in brown paper. Her boss's apartment was only a fifteen-minute brisk walk away and she had delivered things there before. So why not now? She could use the time to contemplate what she would say to her sister when she got home. And she'd also be more relaxed knowing that she'd rectified her mistake and her boss had the right material for his meeting.

Maybe she would even be lucky enough to find his apartment empty so she could swap the incorrect prospectuses with the new ones without him even knowing. Now, that would be a coup she could smile about.

Feeling better than she had all day, she slipped into her suit jacket, grabbed her handbag, and jabbed the lift button to take her to the ground floor.

Being mid-July, Fifth Avenue was teeming with sunburned tourists wearing ill-fitting shorts and weighed down with *I Heart New York* shopping bags.

Weaving in and around them with accustomed dexterity, Cassidy didn't notice that the sky had turned leaden until a large raindrop landed like a burst water balloon right in the centre of her precious parcel.

Groaning with acceptance that this just was not her day, she ducked under a striped shop awning with a couple of women dressed for a night out just as the heavens really opened.

Another drop of water dripped onto her forehead and she barely batted an eyelash as she swiped at it with the back of her hand, glancing up to see a hole in the awning. At this rate a lorry would speed past, hit a puddle, and finish the job. It would only be fitting.

'Excuse me,' one of the women ventured. 'My app's

stopped working. Is Broadway left or right from here? We're late for a show.'

'Left,' Cassidy directed, wishing that getting to Times Square for a musical was the biggest worry on her to-do list right now. In fact, she couldn't remember the last time she'd done anything light-hearted or fun. Who had the time for such frivolities?

Shrugging out of her jacket, she wrapped it around her parcel and hunted around for a cab. Of course the Avenue was gridlocked in the sudden downpour with not a yellow cab in sight.

Resigned to her fate, she stepped out into the deluge, knowing that if she didn't move soon she wouldn't make it home before dark. She only hoped that her boss appreciated her dedication when it came to bonus time.

By the time she made it to his landmark building she was a sodden, out-of-breath mess.

The doorman did a double-take when he saw her and rushed to hold the door open as she dashed inside. 'Evening, Miss Ryan.'

'Evening, Michael.' She paused to catch her breath, her heart racing a mile a minute. 'Is the boss in?'

'Yes, ma'am. He came in an hour ago.'

'Great,' she said glumly. No chance she could hide her mistake, then.

Since he hadn't responded to her earlier text, she used her personal pass to access his penthouse apartment and waited for his private lift.

A sudden attack of nerves hit her as the lift ascended to the top floor. She'd been here on numerous occasions before to drop things off, but she'd never been here when he'd been at home. The thought of seeing him on his home turf made her feel a little jittery, but perhaps that was just a residual feeling from a day she couldn't wait to see the back of.

Arriving in his state-of-the-art apartment with three-hundred-and-sixty-degree views over Manhattan and beyond, she stepped carefully from the elevator so she didn't slip on the marble floor. It was a gorgeous space, the interior designer who had remodelled it having used light wood grain and endless yards of glass to create a home that was boundless and warmly inviting.

Conscious that she was soaking wet, she moved stiffly into the immaculate open-plan living area and called his name. When she didn't get an answer she glanced outside the windows, momentarily captivated by the sunset over heaven-bound skyscrapers. She exhaled slowly, taking in the magnitude and peace of her surroundings. She could see the congested traffic in the distance, the mad dash of pedestrians trying to get to their next destination, and it almost felt surreal in the stillness of Logan's apartment.

After a day that had not let up from morning till now it was like being cocooned in cotton wool, safe from the frantic beat of a city that never slept. A welcome reprieve.

And then suddenly that reprieve was shattered when she felt the air shift behind her. Knowing that it could only be her boss, she gripped her jacket-wrapped parcel tighter and turned, letting out a short gasp when she was confronted by the sight of him. Sweat-soaked in a singlet top that did little to disguise his wide shoulders and ripped torso and tiny gym shorts that hugged his strong thighs, he was a spectacular display of blatant male power and vitality. He had earbuds inserted and she could hear the pounding music from where she stood.

For a moment she couldn't speak, her body frozen by the impact of over six feet of bronzed, honed muscle glistening with athletic prowess. Of course, she'd guessed that he was well built beneath his custommade business suits but her imagination hadn't even come close to the real thing.

Logan's eyes did a slow perusal down her body and she was so out of sorts she felt her insides start to heat up, her heart pumping hard again as if she was still outside, rushing to get out of the rain.

She swallowed heavily, horrified to note that her body was reacting to the sight of him in a way that transcended the professional boss-employee relationship. It had been the same reaction she'd had on first meeting him behind his big desk in a tailored suit and a very bad mood. He hadn't smiled at her then either, testing her mettle by reading her every reaction to his questions with thickly lashed deep blue eyes that were dangerously intelligent.

It was the same look he was giving her now, only this time she didn't feel half as successful at hiding her emotions, something she generally considered one of her superpowers after a childhood fraught with upheaval.

A superpower she had employed within the confines of his office that very first day to hide how attractive she'd found him, concentrating instead on how fortunate she had been to even have the chance at such a prestigious job, and how desperately she had needed the money. It had also helped that there was the somewhat minor—but pivotal—point that a man who already had everything the world had to offer would not give a woman such as herself a second glance.

A bead of water rolled from her forehead down her nose and onto her top lip. Her tongue sneaked out to capture it and Logan's blue eyes darkened, his nostrils flaring as his gaze lingered on her lips. Cassidy felt a surge of sexual awareness so deeply within her body it shook her to the core.

She was like a startled impala facing a hungry lion, with nowhere to run, and she suddenly felt less annoyed at the women who regularly called his office, trying to win a second chance with him, and more sorry for them. If he ever swept her up in those massive arms she wasn't certain she'd want him to let her go either.

Fortunately the scowl that crossed his face was a timely reminder that the chance of him ever sweeping her up into anything was less than zero.

Squeezing her soggy jacket tighter against her chest, she knew that she had to do something to sever this strange connection between them before she embarrassed herself.

But before she had the chance, Logan reached into his pocket and killed the music on his phone before yanking the earbuds out of his ears. 'What are you doing here, Cassidy? And why are you dripping all over my floor?'

They had started using their first names after about six months of working together when he had complained that he felt like she was always about to deliver bad news when she addressed him as Mr de Silva, but now her name sounded strangely intimate on his tongue.

'I…' She crushed the moment of madness she'd just experienced and lifted her chin. 'I need to give you the prospectuses for your meeting tomorrow morning.' She unwrapped the jacket in her arms and held out the package but he didn't move to take it.

'I already have the prospectuses for tomorrow.'

Cassidy grimaced and with her free hand brushed at the rivulets of water rolling down her neck. 'Actually, you don't. You have the wrong ones.'

'Wrong…' His eyes scanned her from head to toe again, a scowl darkening his blue eyes. 'You're drenched.'

'Sorry.' She glanced down to find that her blouse was so wet she might as well have not been wearing one. With a squeak of alarm she crossed her free arm over her breasts, only then realising how terrible she must look in general.

His scowl deepened as he plucked her sodden jacket and the package from her hand and disappeared down the hallway, returning a moment later with a towel.

'You know where the bathroom is,' he bit out, keeping his eyes above her neckline. 'Use it.'

'Actually, I don't,' she said, rubbing her arms from the chill that was either coming from him or the air-conditioning. 'I've only ever dropped things off before and left.'

Clearly annoyed to have his peaceful night invaded, he strode down the hall, impatience evident in every taut line of his hard body. 'Here.'

He pushed open the door to a bathroom and Cassidy gratefully disappeared inside.

She nearly let out another squeak at seeing blotches of mascara pooled beneath her eyes and straggly bits of her hair sticking to her ears and neck.

The ruined woman in the mirror was not the impeccably presented one she had turned herself into since leaving Ohio and it was yet more confirmation that she should not have got out of bed that morning.

Taking a deep breath, she skimmed the towel beneath her eyes and wiped her face and neck. Then she unpinned her hair and searched in her bag for her hairbrush. Not finding it, she had a vague memory of Amber asking if she could borrow it the night before. Cursing her beloved niece, she finger-combed the mass of tangled waves and tried to re-pin her hair. Unfortunately the rain had made it curl in every direction so she gave up, letting it hang past her shoulders. She shivered in the air-conditioned bathroom and groaned anew when she realised that her bra was visible beneath the downlights.

Terrific.

She pulled her blouse away from her skin and wondered if it would look odd if she walked out holding it like that.

Deciding that she'd have to brazen it out, she tilted

her chin and exited the bathroom. She'd get her coat, wish her boss goodnight, and head off to face the next disaster. It couldn't possibly be any worse than this one.

Peeking into the living room, she caught sight of her boss outlined against the New York skyline, his hands on his hips. The clouds had parted and late sunbeams shone down on the newly washed buildings, gilding them in gold and silver.

But it was the gorgeous view inside the room that held her attention more. Tall, broad-shouldered and lean-hipped, with long, muscular legs and dark blond hair that gently curled against his strong neck, he was the epitome of sleek male power in the prime of life. He might be a cold-hearted workaholic but he was pure perfection to look at.

Against her wishes her heart rate quickened once again and, unwilling to get caught staring at him a second time, she turned away to hunt for her jacket.

Logan turned to find Cassidy scanning the room and looking more like something the cat would drag in than his usual efficient EA. All day she'd been off and now she even looked it. Her usually perfect up-do a cloud of chestnut waves, her wet blouse the texture of tissue paper, and just as revealing, and her face clean of make-up. The only thing familiar about her was her glasses, ones she'd adjusted further up her nose with her little finger when she'd caught him staring at her. A nervous gesture he'd only ever seen now and then.

His office ran like clockwork thanks to her. But the

woman standing in front of him looked like she should be about to do a strip tease before ending up in his bed.

Wondering when his libido had regressed to the point that a woman in a wet shirt could turn him on, he strode out of the room and returned with one of his sweatshirts. 'Unless you're planning to enter a wet T-shirt competition after you leave here, you'd better put this on.'

Her eyes didn't quite meet his as she took it from him and slid it over her head, her thanks muffled by the fabric.

The sweatshirt was miles too big, falling midway down her thighs and draping over her hands, but it did the job of turning her from shapely to shapeless as required.

He didn't know what had happened today but it had all started when he had arrived at his office to find that Cassidy wasn't there. Always on time, and with his morning coffee ready for when he walked in, she had been noticeably absent. Not only had he been required to make his own coffee but he'd had to field two visits from junior staff asking for information he didn't have. Then his COO's assistant had stopped by to make an appointment for him to meet with her boss and had tried to linger.

When Cassidy had finally arrived, blaming the subway, she'd been harried. At first he hadn't noticed because she'd appeared as well groomed as always in a black suit and white blouse, her auburn hair pinned back into a French twist. She'd worn it like that on her first day and had never deviated from the style. It had annoyed him at first because it was always the same, but then he'd come to appreciate her consistency. Not to mention her efficiency.

But she hadn't been efficient today. Following up one unexpected mistake with another and another until he'd almost asked her what was wrong.

He hadn't because the last thing he wanted to do was to encourage personal interactions in the office. He did not want to give her any ideas that might change the nature of their working relationship. Something that had happened with more than one EA in the past.

In his experience people were rarely as they seemed on the outside and yet he was sure that his EA was exactly as she seemed: an intelligent, quiet, sensible woman who had incredibly sultry lips. And vivid, velvet-green eyes. He'd noticed both right away, and nearly hadn't hired her because of his reaction to them, but his HR manager had convinced him that she was perfect.

And she had been.

Perfect.

Until now.

She glanced at him and adjusted her glasses again. 'I know you're busy so if you tell me where my jacket is, I'll get out of your hair.'

'Not before you explain why I left the office with the wrong information, you won't.'

She sighed heavily, her chest rising and falling with the effort. 'I was hoping you wouldn't ask.'

Logan raised a brow at her evasive response, another

clue that his EA had left the building and had been replaced by a woman he didn't know.

'Relying on hope is a waste of time and since we don't always get what we want I'll ask again.'

She glanced at her hands before raising her little chin as she looked at him. 'I gave you the draft of the prospectus that was the one before the final copy.' She opened her hands in front of her in a conciliatory gesture. 'I'm not sure how it happened. I did text you to let you know I would be stopping by but clearly you didn't get it.'

'Clearly.' He tried not to be annoyed at her incompetence but he was. 'But I could have collected them from the office in the morning.'

'You have an early flight to Boston and I didn't want to put you out.' She gripped her fingers together. 'It's been a horrible day and I'm really sorry for mucking up.' Her hands lifted in a helpless gesture. 'I'm not myself right now.'

She could join the club. If his unwanted physical reaction to her was any indication, he wasn't himself either. Which was why he needed to retrieve her jacket and send her on her way. About to do exactly that, he frowned when his phone rang. Pulling it from his pocket, his frown deepened when he saw his brother's name flash up on the screen.

Given that it was the middle of the night in Arrantino, it couldn't be good news and he pressed the answer button.

'What?'

His blunt greeting was met with a touch of humour.

'Have I caught you at a bad time, brother? You're not with a woman, are you?'

'Yes.' Before he could think better of it his eyes raked over Cassidy again. She tucked a strand of her hair behind her ear and the innocent gesture sent a raw bolt of primal lust roaring through his blood. Closing it down with ironclad self-control, he turned away from her and corrected his answer. 'No.'

'Good. Have you got a minute? I have…something to tell you.'

Hearing the hesitation in his brother's voice sent an icy shiver of dread down his spine, driving all thoughts of his EA's legs from his mind. 'What is it? Have you been to the doctor? Has—?'

Logan stopped, unable to voice the fear that his brother's teenage leukaemia had returned. Leo had fought the illness bravely but Logan doubted he would ever fully recover from seeing his brother so weakened by the disease. Neither would he forget how powerless he had felt in the face of something he couldn't control.

'No. It's nothing like that,' his brother assured him. 'Well, not entirely. It's just that…' The pause on the end of the phone took ten years off Logan's life. 'I've decided to abdicate. Which makes you the next King of Arrantino.'

CHAPTER TWO

LOGAN'S EYES NARROWED on the darkening sky that stretched for miles outside his window, not sure he'd heard his brother correctly. 'Abdicate?' He ploughed his hand through his sweaty blond hair. 'What the hell are you talking about?'

'An...*issue* has arisen.' His brother sounded pained. 'It wasn't supposed to be like this, to be splashed across the news, but... You know how this works. We live in a goldfish bowl. I wanted it to come out differently but that opportunity has passed.'

'You're not making a bit of sense,' Logan growled. 'Cut to the chase and tell me what's going on.'

'The long and short of it is that Anastasia and I have formally broken up and I'm stepping down.'

'Divorcing your wife is not a reason to abdicate,' Logan said. Especially when divorcing that scheming little predator was the best thing Leo could ever do for himself and his country. The woman had played both of them like a finely tuned instrument five years ago, latching onto the brother who would make her Queen in the end. She had caused a rift between the two of them when Logan had tried to warn Leo against marriage. But her beauty had blinded Leo, and Logan suspected that his brother had also been heavily influenced by his duty as King. Their mother had been in Leo's ear about the need to produce an heir for months before Anastasia had turned up on the scene and the notion had taken root. Unlike Logan, Leo had always tried to do the right thing, rarely questioning his royal duties. Until now, it seemed.

'No, it's not,' Leo agreed. 'But having an affair that has made headline news around the world is.'

'Damn.' Logan swore under his breath. He had never had any hard evidence of Anastasia's affairs, but perhaps she had gone too far this time and finally shown his brother her true colours. 'What has Anastasia done now?' he asked, not even trying to mask the disgust in his voice.

'It's not Anastasia. It's me. And strictly speaking I haven't had an affair because I haven't consummated the relationship yet, but I was photographed kissing another woman and the press are playing it that way, so what does it matter? Mother has hit the roof. The world's press are trying to draw comparisons between myself and Father and are desperate to know who my new love interest is… It's bedlam over here.'

Still processing the fact that his brother was seeing another woman, Logan braced a hand against the window, his muscles rigid. He had no doubt that his mother had hit the roof.

They had all lived in the shadow of their late father's damaging affairs and she had been hurt the most. Both he and his brother had hated his father for it so the fact that Leo had let this happen was shocking enough. The fact that he wanted to abdicate unthinkable.

'Just keep a cool head,' he advised, already working out how he was going to handle the crisis. 'And don't do anything rash. Like abdicate!'

'Too late,' Leo stated without any humour in his voice. 'And actually it's not a rash decision. I made it a month ago. I've just been sitting with it to make sure it's the right one to make.'

'A month ago? Why the hell didn't you call me earlier?'

'Because if it wasn't right I didn't want to bother you. And I knew you'd try to talk me out of it.'

'Damn right I'd have tried to talk you out of it. I wasn't born to be King, you were. And I don't want the job!'

'I had a feeling you'd say that but if you really don't want to do it then we can pass the throne to Ped—'

'Do not even go there,' Logan warned, his throat burning with fury. 'Pedro wouldn't know the first thing about running a country and we both know it.' Their cousin was a surfing maniac who preferred the beach to the boardroom and little else. Except maybe women.

'Yes. But I can no longer fulfil the role. The woman I'm in love with is a single mother who hates the spotlight and—'

'In love?' Logan pushed away from the window, suddenly conscious that Cassidy was still standing in the middle of his living room, nibbling on her lower lip. Dragging his gaze away from those even white teeth, he refocused. 'Are you serious?'

Leo laughed self-consciously. 'I know you think love is little more than sentimental tripe, but it's not. This woman is wonderful. Amazing. I had no idea I could feel this way and all I want to do is protect her and her daughter.'

All Logan wanted to do was stop his brother from doing something stupid. Like abdicate. Because there was no way he wanted to be King. He'd never overly enjoyed the pomp and ceremony and the constant attention that went with royal life, and he really hated the comparisons that were made between him and their late father. As the son who looked most like the old man he'd always borne the brunt of that kind of attention and he'd hated being likened to a man he didn't respect. A man who had chosen to put everything in life—his job, his passions, and his baser instincts—ahead of the welfare of his family and country.

Their father had been a master at manipulation and both he and Leo had gone from loving him to fearing him to turning away from him and, finally, to loathing him. Especially when his affairs had become public knowledge, hurting their mother and embarrassing them all.

And now Leo had fallen into the same trap. Being caught with a woman who wasn't his wife. No matter how innocent it had been, it was still a big deal.

'Just…' He heaved out a sigh. 'Just don't do anything yet. Don't make any solid decisions while you're emotional. And definitely do not put out any statements.' His mind was already turning, working through ideas of how they could stem the fallout from the scandal his brother had inadvertently created. 'I'll be in Arrantino by nightfall. Morning your time.'

'If I'm not here to greet you, I'll make sure Margaux is completely up to speed on what's happening.'

'I don't want to speak to your private secretary,' Logan growled. 'I want to speak to you.'

'I'll try.' Logan could already hear that his brother was distracted.

Ringing off, Logan took a moment to stare into space. King? There was no way he wanted to become King. It was a poisoned chalice he'd always been glad he'd never had to take on.

Cassidy cleared her throat, her gaze taking in her boss's flexed shoulder muscles as he steadied his breathing.

She'd never seen him so disturbed before, and she felt an unexpected shaft of compassion for him. She had felt like she'd had her life turned on its head this morning, and now it seemed like his was about to do the same thing.

He turned toward her, his expression steely. 'How much of that did you get?'

Feeling awful that she'd overheard any of it, she shrugged diffidently. 'Your brother intends to abdicate and you don't want to be King.' *You also think love is a waste of time, and you don't seem to be a fan of your brother's soon-to-be ex-wife.*

'That's pretty much it. Throw in a divorce, a woman on the side, and a hungry pack of journalists and you've potentially got a national crisis.'

'Wow. And I thought my morning had been bad. What are you going to do?'

'Talk him out of it.'

Cassidy sighed. 'You always seem to know what your next move is. One of the things I admire most about you is your ability to make a decision on the spot. I wish that was one of my superpowers.'

'Superpower?'

'Things I excel at.'

'Your superpower is running my office. Which I'm going to need you to get on top of right away because we need to fly to Arrantino. Tonight. Hopefully we're only looking at a twenty-four-hour turnaround but you'll need to rearrange the rest of my week in case it's not.'

'Okay, right.' She frowned. 'I'll send an email to postpone tomorrow's meeting in Boston. Then first thing tomorrow I'll see what can be delegated and what has to be rearranged. Do you want me to call Ben to reschedule the flight?'

'I already sent him a text requesting that we fly out as soon as he can log a new flight plan.'

'Okay, then I'll…' Cassidy paused. That was the second time she'd heard him refer to both of them. 'We?'

'Yes.' Logan checked an incoming text on his phone. 'I need you to come with me.'

Cassidy blinked as her brain slowly processed his words. 'But I can't go with you.'

Logan's head snapped up. He looked at her as if she'd never said no to him before, perhaps because she hadn't. 'Why not?'

She thought about the conversation she still needed to have with her sister, and her obligation to take care of the twins two evenings a week while her sister studied at night school. 'I have obligations. Commitments.' She smoothed her hand over her sodden hair. And if this trip did by chance go longer than twenty-four hours her sister wouldn't be happy. Not with her final exams about to start.

'Yes, you do have commitments. To me. And right now I need you.'

'You need me to run your office, which I can do better from New York.'

'I decide where you're best fit to serve me, Cassidy, not you.'

Up until now Cassidy would have said that she didn't have a temper, but she was so exhausted from all the issues she'd had to contend with today that she could feel it rising. And not once in the time she had worked for him had he ever spoken to her in such an imperious tone. It made her think of a spoiled, rich prince getting everything he wanted. Which no doubt he had done.

Having grown up in the opposite of the lap of luxury, she couldn't even imagine how it would feel to have every one of your needs met whenever you desired it. Unfortunately her boss didn't share that experience. Which was no doubt why he showed so little emotion whenever one of his ex-girlfriends rang up begging for a second chance. Which he never gave. Once you were off Logan de Silva's list of intimate contacts, you were off. From what she had seen, he was a man who cared very little about anything other than winning his next billion-dollar deal, and she sometimes envied him that because she cared too much about everything.

'Well, I'm sorry but I can't just drop everything to be at your beck and call. When I first started working for you I explained that I would need advance notice if you ever needed me to travel with you.' Which so far he hadn't. 'And leaving to go halfway around the world in five minutes hardly counts as even short notice.'

'And might I remind you,' he said with lethal softness, 'that when you signed on as my EA I explained that I pay above and beyond the average wage because I specifically require you to be at my beck and call, and you were more than happy with that at the time.'

The dark look in his eyes made her feel hot and bothered. She was still uncomfortably aware that he was standing in front of her half-naked, her eyes constantly drawn to the pelt of dark hair that curled over the top of his singlet. She couldn't seem to stop herself from imagining how he would look naked.

She was also uncomfortably aware that what he said was true. But all she could think about was how she was going to tell Peta that she wouldn't be around this week when her sister had to take her final exams. It must be another one of Murphy's laws that when something horrible happened, it happened at the worst possible time.

Silence stretched between them with such savage intensity it completely took the wind out of her sails. She'd never been good with confrontation, which was why she was so good in her role as peacemaker in her family. It was her other superpower, along with her ability to compartmentalise situations and move on.

Knowing by his expression that he wouldn't take no for an answer, she grimaced. 'You're right, I did agree with your requirements when I took the job, but...' She faced him as one might face an angry lion in a small enclosure without a whip or a chair. 'I'll have to make a call first. Peta needs me more than ever this week.'

Logan came toward her, all power and languid grace, and for a moment she didn't think he was going to stop. Her eyes widened as she was assailed with the unexpected vision of him wrapping one of those large hands around the back of her neck and drawing her up on her toes to kiss her. Heat travelled swiftly up through her body, making her tingle in all the wrong places.

Breathless, she waited for what would no doubt be the kiss of her life to happen, but of course it didn't. He stopped an inch from touching her. 'As I said, so do I.' The look he gave her could have cut glass. All signs of the vulnerability she had glimpsed when he'd been speaking to his brother had completely disappeared. 'And my needs take precedence over Peter's. I'll have Gordon drop you home so you can shower and change and then I'll collect you in an hour. Be ready.'

His gaze flicked slowly down over her body and back up and Cassidy became very conscious that she must look like the Wicked Witch of the West with her hair drying in clumps and wearing one of his sweat-shirts that was miles too big for her.

Then he was gone, leaving her to stew in silence.

She wondered if he was ever like this with his dates. But if he was they wouldn't be crying on the end of the phone when he broke up with them, they'd be rejoicing.

Like this he was domineering and exacting. There was only one way and that was his. Usually she didn't mind it. Usually she went with it.

Usually when she didn't feel like her life was falling apart at the seams. It made her want to tell him just where he could take his demanding attitude and what he could do with it when he got there. Which would shock the heck out of him because, while he encouraged her to give him her opinion on matters of business, he would never encourage her to outwardly defy him.

And she was sure if that ever happened he'd be the juggernaut he always was, speeding over whatever roadblocks were in his way like a souped-up supercar. Cassidy, by comparison, was more like a moped, dodging life's pitfalls as best she could with only one cylinder.

Logan stepped into the shower and doused his head under a stream of hot water. He didn't know what had shocked him more, the fact that Cassidy had said no to him or that she had a lover called Peter.

A shaft of something akin to jealousy speared through him and he knew why that was. She was the best EA he'd ever had. There was no way he wanted her falling in love, getting married, going off to have babies and leaving him.

Was she already in love with the guy? Is that why

she was so keen to leave on time two nights a week and baulked at working weekends?

He thought about the way her bright green eyes had widened as he'd invaded her personal space. For a moment he'd been overcome with the urge to keep going and power her back against the wall until he had her flattened against him, and the intensity of that urge had been the only thing that had stopped him.

Had she felt the inconvenient chemistry between them?

Had she wanted him to claim her?

Logan swore softly and stuck his head back under the stream of water, turning it to an icy blast.

He had not found himself at the mercy of his baser instincts since he'd learned that giving in to passion and losing control was what had nearly brought his father unstuck. It was certainly what had eventually broken them as a family. Even calling themselves a family was a stretch. They'd been an institution that had performed for the public like trained seals, both parents putting duty ahead of everything else.

And he wouldn't ruin things with the best EA he'd ever had by confusing desire with a heightened state of adrenaline. Which was all that had been.

First the shock of finding her in his apartment like a half-drowned kitten and then being confronted with all that gloriously wild hair he'd itched to bury his fingers in. Who knew she'd been hiding that from the world?

Did she hide it from Peter as well, or just him?

Why do you care?

Irritated to find his mind once again charging down

a path he had no intention of allowing it to go, he put the brakes on all thoughts of Cassidy's unruly appearance. It had happened, but it was over.

The sooner he saw her again in her usual sedate office attire the sooner he could forget he'd ever seen her any other way.

Professional. Sensible. Unflappable.

So no more imagining himself peeling open her lacy bra. No more wondering if her hair would be silky soft beneath his fingertips. And definitely no more arousing himself by wondering how her body would fit against his as he pressed himself into her.

Like now.

Cursing again, he pulled on jeans and a pullover and questioned his instinctive decision to take her with him to Arrantino. Perhaps she would be better staying back here in his office, taking care of business while he was gone.

But as soon as the thought formed he discounted it. The fact was he needed Cassidy with him because he had no idea what he was about to face, or how long he'd be gone. He was hoping it would only be a twenty-four-hour turnaround. Fly in, drum some sense into his brother, say hello to his mother, and fly out. Simple. Easy.

But if for some reason simple turned to complicated it would be far more efficient to have Cassidy with him than sending urgent messages to a different time zone and wondering how long it would be before she processed them.

But for that to happen she had to be completely on her game. She had to be back to her usual measured self.

And for that matter, so did he.

In her own words it had been a horrible day, capped off with a horrible night. His current adrenaline rush had nothing to do with Cassidy and everything to do with his brother's announcement that he wanted to abdicate. He wouldn't, Logan would see to that, but it had thrown him. Put him in in a heightened state of awareness. Like a warrior of old about to go into battle. All his senses were switched on and that was the only reason he had felt any form of arousal for Cassidy.

Feeling as if he had everything in hand again, he organised a change of clothes for himself and texted his driver to see if he'd returned to pick him up. The sooner he got to Arrantino and back, the better.

CHAPTER THREE

CASSIDY HAD TO jiggle her key in the lock a bit to open the old door of her clapboard rental and when she did she found the twins doing their homework on the coffee table, watching the latest reality singing show.

They waved an absent-minded hello, their eyes glued to the TV, as Peta came out of the kitchenette, wiping her hands on a dishrag. 'You're late tonight. I was getting worried.'

'Sorry. I sent a text.'

'An hour ago.' Peta followed her into the bedroom. 'Is everything okay? You look like you've just climbed out of someone's bed. And whose sweatshirt are you wearing?'

She had almost forgotten the shirt and blushed even though there was no reason to. 'It's Logan's.'

'Your boss?' Peta frowned as Cassidy reached into her closet and pulled her ancient suitcase down from the shelf. 'Why are you wearing your boss's shirt, and where are you going?'

'Arrantino.'

'For how long?'

Cassidy glanced over at her sister's disgruntled expression as she quickly folded a work blouse into her suitcase. 'I don't know. A day or two.'

'A day or two?' Peta frowned. 'I need you to take care of the girls this week. I'm in the middle of my final exams.'

'I know.' Cassidy hated that she was putting her sister out, and she genuinely loved taking care of her nieces. 'I thought maybe Dan could do it if I'm not back. Or Miss Marple across the hall.' Not that the twins liked her very much, other than when they deliberately confused her by pretending to be each other. 'I'm really sorry, but there's nothing I can do.'

'There is.' Her sister slapped her hands on her hips. 'You could say no.'

Cassidy thought about reminding Peta that her job as Logan de Silva's assistant was the only reason they could afford to pay their current rent, and the reason Peta had been able to attend beauty school while paying for her twins to get a decent education, but didn't. She didn't want Peta to feel guilty about Cassidy providing for them financially when she genuinely loved her job, and her sister and her twin nieces even more.

'You don't say no to Logan de Silva,' she said.

'Then quit. You initially took the job in the bank because it paid so well, but you're not really utilising your project management degree to the fullest. Maybe you should put some feelers out to see where that can take you.'

And one day she would. She'd move on from this job and expand her professional scope but that time wasn't when she might have to trawl through real-estate ads looking for a new place to live.

'You know your boss says jump and you say how high?' Peta added. 'And you still haven't explained why you're wearing his shirt.' Her sister gave her an assessing look. 'There's nothing going on between you, is there?'

'Of course not!' The very idea was a joke. 'I'm wearing his shirt because I got caught in the rain.'

'Thank God.' Peta exhaled a relieved breath. 'I don't want to see you get hurt.'

The fact that her sister thought she would be the one to get hurt in such a preposterous scenario stung a little. 'Maybe he would be the one left broken-hearted,' she said loftily.

'Get real.' Peta laughed, folding a skirt Cassidy had placed on the bed and adding it to her suitcase. 'He's a prince and a billionaire. I think we both know who would come out worst if anything did happen between you.'

And that stung a lot. It wasn't as if she harboured any secret illusions where her illustrious boss was concerned. She knew he was out of her league. And really she wasn't even sure she wanted to meet anyone. The few times she had dated had been a disaster she didn't care to repeat.

But for Peta to also just assume that she wasn't capable of attracting a man like Logan if she actually wanted to hurt more than it should. She'd sustained her sister in every way that she could over the years and a little bit of support in return wouldn't go astray.

'Lucky I'm not that foolish,' she said, blindly grabbing underwear from a drawer.

'Just be careful,' Peta cautioned. 'I've heard the way your voice changes when you talk about him and it worries me. You've been so content to do his bidding since you started working for him and I've sometimes wondered if you're not a little bit in love with him, Cass.'

'In love...?' Cassidy zipped her suitcase closed with a little more force than necessary. 'That's absurd.' She wasn't in love with her boss. If she was ever going to fall in love she wanted it to be with someone she had half a chance of being with, not with a prince who had an appetite for supermodels. Being five feet five and homely, that wouldn't be her.

She sighed. How did things change so quickly? Yesterday she'd gone to work, stopped at the dojo where she practised martial arts for two hours twice a week and helped the twins with their maths homework after dinner. Her private life ran as seamlessly as her professional life and she was happy with it. There were no complications and no nasty surprises waiting around the corner.

Peta gave her a look. 'Your problem is that you're always too willing to help the underdog and it will come back to bite you one day.'

Cassidy laughed and shook her head. 'If there is one thing Logan de Silva cannot be described as, it's an underdog.'

'I was speaking metaphorically,' Peta dismissed.

'But he plays to your sense of obligation and I don't want him to take advantage of you.'

Perhaps he wasn't the only one who did that, she reflected, instantly contrite at the unbidden thought. Her sister was beautiful and wilful but she was also loyal and loving.

'Just don't be a pushover,' Peta continued. 'You deserve more for yourself. You deserve to have a life other than work and me and the twins. It's something to think about.'

Cassidy felt her hackles rise at the underlying message in her sister's tone. 'I have a life. And I love taking care of my nieces.'

'Yes, but you don't have anything else.'

'I don't need anything else,' she said, struggling not to feel testy at her sister's insistence. 'Look, I can't stand here and argue with you right now. I need to grab a shower, change, and do my hair before he arrives to collect me. And, yes, I know that makes me a pushover in your eyes but…'

Right now she didn't feel as if she had any choice. Logan had made it clear that she had to go with him and unless she was prepared to lose her job—which she wasn't at the moment—she could hardly defy him.

A shiver went through her as she recalled that moment in his apartment when she'd seen him standing there half-naked, dripping in sweat. It was as if she'd never seen such a thing before. She had. Plenty of times at her dojo.

The last person she wanted to find attractive was her boss. And hopefully the feeling was an aberration, the result of stress, and would be completely gone by the time she joined him in the car.

Noticing that Peta was still watching her with a frown on her face, Cassidy lifted her chin. 'I'll be fine. I'm always fine.'

But half an hour later, as Dan carried her case to the front door, she didn't feel fine.

'Don't worry about the girls,' he said, giving her shoulder a light squeeze as he leaned down to kiss her cheek. 'I'll look out for them while you're gone.'

Cassidy murmured her appreciation as he handed Logan's driver her suitcase. She especially didn't feel fine as she followed Gordon down the short walkway and climbed into the back of the town car. She felt more of a pushover than ever.

Her sister's comments kept replaying in her head, particularly the one about her being secretly in love with her boss, as she glanced over to find him sprawled in the back of the car like a disgruntled model wearing faded jeans and a knit sweater that hugged his muscular frame. She really wished that he didn't look so good because she couldn't deny that the flashes of sexual chemistry she'd felt in his apartment earlier had seriously unsettled her. Particularly since they hadn't gone away as she'd hoped. It was as if seeing him half-naked had revealed a deep-seated desire inside herself she hadn't even known she possessed. And she needed to close it down. Now.

Despite what Peta said, she was happy with her life. She didn't need anything else, and she wasn't about to jeopardise her job by making the fatal error of creating more out of this unwanted attraction to her boss than actually existed. Today was just one of those days and tomorrow she'd be back to normal. Until then she'd grit her teeth and focus on work.

'Why are you wearing a suit?'

His voice was low and smooth in the confines of the darkened car.

Cassidy glanced at him. 'Because we're going on a business trip.' And, in her view, clothes maketh the person.

Growing up in a small, conservative parish, you soon learned that the way you dressed mattered a lot. She knew what it meant to be gossiped about and turned into an outcast. After their mother had deserted them Peta had become a bit of a wild child, running with the wrong crowd and falling pregnant by the town rebel at sixteen. The townsfolk had gone from supportive to vitriolic, and in the blink of an eye the Ryan girls were bad news. Then Cassidy had inadvertently added to their newfound notoriety in a way that had seemed to solidify her family's reputation in the eyes of their town.

She still remembered how devastating it had felt to walk down the street and know that everyone was whispering about you behind your back. Their father had lost his job, having to find work in a nearby parish, leaving her and Peta alone for long periods of time.

Finally they had moved and things had slowly improved, but with twin babies to clothe and feed, they had all gone into survivor mode. During that time Cassidy had vowed to step out of the mould she'd been placed in so that now, when people met her, they saw the smart, capable woman that she was and not the downtrodden girl she had once been.

'It's late,' Logan said, dragging her mind out of the past she'd left behind. 'And we'll be flying all night. I don't expect you to be uncomfortable.'

'I won't be.' And even if she was she'd never let him know.

Wondering if she was going to get anything right today, she pulled her tablet out of her bag to check her emails. What she needed to do was think of this unexpected trip to Arrantino as a godsend because it would give her a chance to work up a plan and think clearly about her next move.

Because no matter how much she hated the thought of it, her sister was moving out and Cassidy had no clue as to what she would do next. She couldn't afford to live alone, but the thought of getting a new flatmate depressed her. What if the person she chose turned out to be a weirdo? Or what if things didn't work out between Peta and Dan? Perhaps she should remain alone in case her sister and the twins needed to move back in again. The whole situation made her feel vulnerable and rejected—two emotional states she worked very hard to avoid.

Just as she had worked hard to help her sister out, upgrading to a larger place when Peta and the twins had moved to New York so she could be on hand to support them. Peta had barely been able to make ends meet since the twins had been born and as Cassidy had been finishing an online degree at Colombia, it had made sense for them to all move in together.

But she really wanted to ask Peta if she was sure about Dan. After she'd had the twins Peta had vowed to never trust another man again. She'd devoted herself to bringing up her girls and giving them a stable life and, okay, maybe it had been short-sighted to think that Peta would never meet another man again, but Cassidy had believed her when she'd said she was done with men. They had even joked that if there were any good men left in the world they wouldn't come near the Ryan sisters.

'Are you planning to turn that on, or just stare at it the whole time?'

Cassidy blinked, embarrassed to discover that she had become so engrossed by memories of the past that she had yet to turn on her device. 'I had an argument with Peta,' she admitted with a slight grimace. 'It's distracted me.'

Logan's brow climbed his forehead. 'Over you coming with me, I presume.'

'Yes.'

'You did explain that it's just business.'

'Of course,' she said briskly. 'But apparently I'm always putting work ahead of my social life. It's unhealthy.'

'Peter sounds a little demanding. I hope this isn't going to interfere with your work.'

'Not at all.'

Although hadn't Peta's announcement about her

engagement been the thing to put her in a spin in the first place?

Logan must have noted something in her expression because he scowled. 'You had better be sure because I need you to be your usual self while we're in Arrantino.'

'I know you're referring to how many times I mucked up today,' she said, 'but that was out of the ordinary.'

'I want ordinary.'

Well, if there was an annual award for Miss Ordinary she'd win it uncontested. 'You've got it.' She gave him a tight smile.

Despite the lateness of the hour, Republic Airport was busy and noisy as Gordon drove the car straight onto the tarmac. A light plane was about to land, and a jeep sped out of a nearby hangar to greet it. Another plane was set to take off and closer at hand a small black helicopter sat like a squat beetle, its rotors suddenly whining and whipping up the air around them.

Cassidy ducked her head against the downdraught, moving quickly toward the set of airstairs connected to Logan's private plane. Strands of her hair had come loose from the downdraught and she pushed them back, missing one of the steps as she did so.

Logan immediately clamped his strong hand around her elbow, sending a bolt of sensation up her arm.

Disturbed by even that small touch, Cassidy thanked him and quickly scrambled to ascend the stairs.

Taking in the plush leather interior in one quick glance, she settled into one of the armchairs by the window, buckled her seat belt and handed a customs official her passport to check.

Once they were cleared to fly, Logan took the seat on the other side of the glossy table from her.

Ignoring the way her heart sped up, she scrolled through her boss's schedule and fired off a few quick emails, cancelling the most obvious meetings.

Then she worked through the various emails on her tablet. So far there were none relating to the scandal in Arrantino, but Cassidy knew that it was just a matter of time. 'Once we're airborne we'll need to go over my schedule for the week and decide which meetings to delegate and which ones to cancel.'

'I've already worked that out,' she said without looking up. 'I'm just not sure what to do with the stakeholder meeting for the new Westgate tunnel development on Thursday morning. It's still two days away so we can wait, but I don't want to cancel at the last minute because there's a very real chance that the Peterstone Organisation will get cold feet and pull out before then.'

Which would undermine the whole process, not to mention render all the work they had done winning over the relevant Australian government agencies over the last eight months to be the front runners to win the bid to build the new tunnel. It was a ten-billion-dollar deal, but they needed the equity that the Peterstone Organisation was looking to invest to cover the debt. She knew it was an important deal to Logan because it would launch the Arrantino bank into a whole new market.

Everyone had said that he wouldn't be able to pull it off, which had only made him work harder, and she'd hate to see all that effort go to waste.

'If they pull out because I can't make it then they pull out,' he said dismissively. 'The future of my country is more important than one deal.'

Knowing he was downplaying how disappointed he was at the prospect of losing the coup, she nodded. 'I'll draft a response and put it on hold until you've had a chance to speak with your brother.' Her fingers flew effortlessly across the keyboard, only pausing when the plane set off down the runway.

Cassidy glanced out the window and gripped the armrests with both hands.

'Are you a nervous flyer?'

Unaware that Logan had been watching her, she glanced up, a wide smile curving her lips. 'No.' She sounded breathless, a warm buzzing feeling in her stomach as the jet rocketed down the runway. 'I love flying. Particularly take-off. I've only ever flown once before and I don't want to miss a single part of it.'

Peta had won an all-expenses-paid trip to Cancun on the radio after arriving in New York and for one blissful week she, Peta, and the twins had soaked up the sun and sipped mocktails by the swimming pool. It had definitely given Cassidy the travel bug, but since then she'd had little time or money to set aside for holidays.

Suddenly the plane lifted off and her stomach bottomed out. 'Does it always feel that way?'

'I don't know,' Logan said with a frown. 'I barely take any notice any more.'

'Well, I definitely want to experience that again.'
She released a rushed breath, and then coloured when
she noticed the frown on his face. 'Sorry. You're probably used to travelling with women who are a lot more
sophisticated. Shall we get back to work?'

'Actually, it's probably best if you turn in and get
some sleep. There's a bedroom at the rear of the plane.
You can use that.'

Cassidy could feel the weight of the whole day bearing down on her and she groaned softly when she mentally went through the clothing she had packed and
realised that she had been so distracted by her discus-
sion with Peta that she hadn't packed anything to sleep
in. In fact, the only thing other than suits and clean
underwear she had packed was her dobok, and she'd
only grabbed that because it had been lying on the end
of the bed freshly laundered. She hadn't even packed
a change of shoes.

As if sensing her frustration, Logan glanced up from
the reports he had spread out on the table. 'What's
wrong?'

Reluctant to go into the specifics, she shrugged
lightly. 'I forgot to pack something to sleep in.'

His eyes caught and held hers for a moment. 'I have
plenty of shirts on board, you can use one of those.'

'No, that's fine.' She already borrowed an item of
his clothing today and it was more than enough. 'Just
tell me how many hours are left in this day.'

'Two.'

'I think I'm going to sit here and count the seconds
before I move again. I swear I must have walked under

a ladder or a black cat crossed my path this morning without me noticing it.'

His brow quirked. 'You're superstitious?'

'No.' She sighed heavily. 'But how else do you account for a day like today?'

Logan's lips curled into a rueful grin. 'You roll with it.'

That is exactly what her sensei would tell her to do.

'Easy for some,' she said despondently. 'I'm not a roll-with-it kind of girl.' She never had been and she never would be. 'I'm more the pull it apart, analyse it to death and put it into a plastic food container kind of girl. That's why your office runs so well.'

And maybe why her love life sucked. She'd discovered on the few dates that she'd had that men generally didn't appreciate being picked apart so that their motives were laid bare. Unfortunately for them, Cassidy didn't like being used so it inevitably turned into a lose-lose situation.

'My office hasn't run quite so well today,' Logan drawled.

'I know. And again I'm sorry about that. I had a few things on my mind.'

'Such as?'

Cassidy blinked with surprise, absently noting the granite-hard line of his unshaven jaw. She had never seen him as anything other than clean-shaven in the office and she couldn't stop herself from wondering if it would be hard or soft to the touch. 'You really want to know?'

'If it means I have my EA back then I do.'

For a moment she had thought that he'd actually been interested in her as a person and now she felt... disappointed. Wondering whether to tell him or not, she decided that he had asked and, knowing him, he'd likely push until she answered anyway.

'My sister told me that she's getting married and it threw me out all day.'

Logan frowned. 'You don't like her partner?'

'No, I love him. He's great...but she... It's just taken me by surprise. And on top of that she needed me to look after my twin nieces this week so she's not happy with me for leaving.'

'Can't she find someone else?'

'I'm hoping she can, but really I look after them all the time so we've never had to rely on anyone else on a regular basis.'

'All the time?'

Seeing his surprise, she shrugged. 'Pretty much. But I'm always happy to do it. I love my nieces.'

'I'm sure you do. But it sounds like your sister is taking advantage.'

Having felt guilty for thinking the same thing herself once or twice, Cassidy jumped to Peta's defence. 'She's had a hard time. She was a teenage mother and the twin's father bailed before they were born. She didn't have a lot of help and it was really hard for her.'

'I have no doubt. So who did help out?' he asked shrewdly. 'You?'

'There wasn't anyone else. Our mother had left two years earlier, and our father sort of lost the plot. He became depressed and started gambling...' She bit into her lower lip as she remembered how worried she and

Peta had been that something would happen to him. That fear had been realised when a few years back he'd died after his car had collided with a tree.

'Logan, I'm pretty sure you don't want to hear any of this.' And she was shocked to find that she was seriously at risk of blurting out her long, sordid history, including her own awful indiscretion, and she never talked about the past to anyone, preferring to leave it long buried. 'I promise that once we land I'll be back to normal. In fact, I'll start now. I'm going to sit here and work all night then my lack of packing won't matter.'

'You can't do that. We'll arrive just before lunch Arrantinian time tomorrow and I need you fresh. If you don't sleep you'll suffer jet-lag.'

'I'll be fine.'

Logan sat back in his chair, regarding her steadily. 'I didn't know you were this stubborn.'

'I'm not stubborn.'

'Cassidy, if I have to order you into the bedroom, I will.'

Cassidy's eyes went wide. She blushed, even though she knew there was no reason to. Still the devil on her shoulder whispered to her that she should ask him what he would do if she disobeyed and the heated anticipation that shot through her sent her flying to her feet.

'Fine. I'll use the bed. But I'm not borrowing a shirt.'

Not waiting for his response, she grabbed her bag and suitcase and went in search of the bedroom.

Logan released a slow breath after Cassidy headed out of sight and scrubbed his hand over his face.

He was very glad that she hadn't taken up the offer

of his shirt. Just the thought of her in that and nothing else had been enough to send his blood pressure sky high again. But what would she be wearing instead? Her underwear? Nothing?

Cursing beneath his breath as his body responded with predictable urgency, he ripped the cap off the nearest water bottle and guzzled the liquid to cool himself down.

When Cassidy had stepped into his car dressed in a suit, and with her hair fastidiously tied back, despite his questioning of her, he'd breathed a sigh of relief that his normal EA had returned, but she kept doing things that threw him off centre.

Like her excitement over the plane taking off. She'd been right when she'd said she'd come across as unsophisticated. None of the other women he dated would have ever shown such a natural reaction, always carefully considering how they looked before opening their mouths, and to his disbelief he'd found himself enjoying Cassidy's uncensored delight.

He'd enjoyed her smile even more. It had transformed her face from attractive to stunning and he'd been unable to look away. It was as if he'd never seen the woman smile before and with a frown he realised that he couldn't remember a time when he had. Not like that, anyway. She came to work, she did her job, and then she went home. It was the way he liked it and the way he wanted it to remain.

Wondering if she was as innocent in other matters as she was in flying, Logan gave himself a mental dressing down. He recognised that he was probably only seeking a distraction from thinking about his current problems, but his EA was off limits. Besides, she already had a lover. The tall, well-built guy who had kissed her goodbye in her doorway. So not that innocent after all.

His jaw clenched at the thought of her with some unknown man, and he didn't like the way that affected him either. Cassidy could be with ten men and it wouldn't have anything to do with him.

Reminding himself that he might be his father's son but he most definitely did not behave like him with his employees, he forced his mind to forget Cassidy's sweet smile and instead think about the more important issue of what he was going to say to his brother after he arrived in Arrantino.

He also reminded himself that Cassidy's childhood was none of his business and that he did not get personal with his EAs. Personal equalled complicated and complicated equalled trouble. All he needed to know about Cassidy was whether she was fit enough to do her job, not how she had coped with all the difficulties she had obviously faced.

He rolled his shoulders and felt the muscles in his back bunch and release. Maybe his sudden interest in her was not only to do with shock, but because he didn't want to think about going home. Going home to face the restricted life of a sitting monarch.

Not if he could help it.

It was enough to sometimes feel that he was like his father, a man who had always been in control of his surroundings—Logan certainly didn't want to return and take up the same job that he had held. But he also knew that he'd do anything for his brother after watching him battle so much to be well. It left him in quite a dilemma.

Unbidden, his gaze shifted to the rear of the plane. To Cassidy. He scrubbed a hand over his face, resigned to the fact that it was going to be a long night.

CHAPTER FOUR

ARRANTINO WAS BEAUTIFUL.

Cassidy couldn't take her eyes off the landscape she could see from her vantage point in the plane as they were coming in to land. High mountains and deep green valleys and villages dotted outside the main city, which looked to have a wall running around the perimeter and a river winding through it. Not that she could see it all, but she could see that it was nestled on the coast and the sand looked like a ribbon of gold against the deep blue of the Mediterranean.

A blue the exact shade of Logan's eyes.

Not that she should be thinking about his eyes. Or any other part of his anatomy, for that matter. Today was a new day and it was going to be the exact opposite of the day before.

To her surprise she'd managed to sleep most of the night in the hugely comfortable bed and she was showered and dressed for success, as the twins would say.

In the end she'd slept in her knickers and blouse and it had been okay. With any luck Logan would sort out this issue with his brother quickly and they'd be back home by tonight New York time before she even needed to launder anything.

She wondered what was behind Logan's staunch determination that he would not be King. She could guess that some of it had to do with the fact that he didn't want to change his life and maybe he didn't want to move back to Arrantino, but his comment that he wasn't king material had made her curious.

If anyone was king material, in her mind, it was her boss. He commanded attention and respect wherever he went, without even trying, and people lined up to get his advice. Admittedly that advice was usually business related but she didn't believe for a second that his keen intelligence was limited to running a bank. Especially since he'd completely turned it around in the five years he'd been at the helm and lifted it from just another boutique investment bank into a global concern. His reach into the Australasian market was the last bastion he had to conquer and she knew he wouldn't rest until he had, and he would because he worked harder than any person she'd ever met before.

His determination was a formidable force and she was only glad it was his brother who had to face it and not her.

The image of him stalking toward her in his apartment building as he'd told her that his needs took precedence over Peta's sent a hot, shivery sensation down her spine, pooling low in her pelvis. Which did not bode well for the business-as-usual front she planned to adopt.

The last thing she had ever wanted was to find her

boss sexually attractive and for those few moments, and a few afterwards when she'd caught the look in his eyes, that was how she had felt.

And it didn't seem to matter that he was exactly the kind of man her dear father had warned her and Peta away from when they had hit their teenage years. Men who were too good looking for their own good, and expected everything to drop into their laps. Cassidy wasn't sure if Logan expected it, or if it just happened because of who he was, but there was no doubt that it did happen. Her sister's question about whether she was in love with him returned like a bomb. But she wasn't in love with Logan, just her job.

A job she relied on too much to ever put it in jeopardy by developing feelings for her boss. Her world had fallen apart before, and now, with her sister throwing in the curveball of her impending marriage, it was more imperative than ever that Cassidy keep at least one aspect of her life the same. Because while most people could deal with change relatively easily, the whole concept of it made her want to run for the hills.

Feeling skittish about what lay ahead, she went online on her laptop and did another check on what was being reported, to find that not only was news of the King's affair being bandied around but the breaking news was that he planned to abdicate as well.

Cassidy knew how much Logan would hate this new development. How much he would hate being critiqued and analysed by the world's media. And no doubt it would make his conversation with his brother that much more difficult. But would it make the King more or less inclined to abdicate? And what would that mean for her if Logan did become King? Would she keep working for him? Would he want her to? Would she want to?

Not wanting to think about any of that, she shoved all thoughts of her family and the changes afoot in her life to the back of her mind and concentrated on the information in front of her. From what she could see, the palace had not yet commented on the growing crisis, but in her estimation they would need to do so soon. Already the London Stock Exchange had responded to the news of the King's imminent abdication with a downward turn of Arrantinian stock, and no doubt New York would follow suit when it opened.

In addition, the paparazzi were trying even harder to find out the identity of the petite brunette seen in the King's arms and Cassidy was only glad it wasn't her.

She knew how it felt to have everyone talking about you behind your back and she never wanted to go through that again.

Wondering where her boss was now that they were so close to landing, she looked up to see him walking toward her.

Freshly showered and shaved, with his honey-blond hair scraped back from his forehead and wearing a crisp navy suit with a pale blue shirt that highlighted his olive skin, he looked like a man who could give a woman a night of endlessly hot sex.

And since when did she start her mornings thinking about sex, endless or otherwise?

She swallowed heavily, and sternly reminded herself

that wide shoulders and a powerful physique were the least important attributes that made a man desirable. A caring nature and a good sense of humour were far more favourable.

Unfortunately those traits didn't even rate as he sprawled in the seat opposite her like a model, his brilliant blue eyes scanning her face as he picked up the espresso the co-pilot had not long since delivered. 'What's wrong?'

'Why do you think something is wrong?' she parried.

'You're staring.'

'Oh, I...' She sucked in a deep breath and forcibly shut down the disastrous attraction she was struggling to get on top of. There was the much more pressing issue of the conjecture surrounding Leo's abdication to inform him of. 'I think you need to brace yourself.'

Logan stretched out his long legs beneath the table, taking up most of the space. 'Just give it to me straight.'

'The media have picked up the story that Leo is thinking of abdicating, pretty much the whole world now knows.'

Logan didn't move a muscle as he looked at her, his thickly lashed gaze narrowing dangerously. 'Perhaps next time I say give it to me straight, don't listen.' He let out a frustrated breath and massaged his forehead. 'Anything else?'

'Arrantinian stock has fallen four percent in London this morning and there's intense speculation as to whether you will become King or not.'

'Let them speculate.' The dangerous look in his eyes

deepened and he suddenly pushed to his feet and paced around the cabin. 'It's what they do best. Lying in wait for one of us to slip up.'

Cassidy grimaced. 'Todd Greene is also one of the journalists on the story.' And she knew how her boss would take that news and he didn't disappoint, cursing volubly under his breath.

Todd Greene had been searching for dirt on Logan for three years now. Ever since Logan had insisted that he be fired from a respected newspaper for writing a salacious story about an actress Logan had dated that had ended with her checking into rehab. Todd had struggled to find work after that and as a result he had promised that he'd get Logan back. So far he'd come up empty.

'From his article I get the feeling he's either in Arrantino or on his way,' she added, frowning as she scanned an article questioning the King's health.

'What is it?' Having noticed her hesitation, Logan's interest sharpened to that of a sword tip.

'I'm not sure. There's something here about your brother's illness returning.'

She glanced up in time to see a flash of pain cross her boss's face. 'It hasn't,' he said woodenly. 'Leo is fine.'

Cassidy knew very little about his brother. She'd never had any inclination to delve into Logan's royal history so she hadn't. But she knew all about what it felt like to have people whisper about you behind your back and she wouldn't wish it on anyone. 'What did he have?'

Logan arched a brow at her question. 'You mean you haven't done an Internet search on my background already?'

'No.' She could sense his anger from across the enclosed space and some deep-seated part of her wanted to reach across the small distance and sooth him. 'Should I have done?'

He gave a harsh bark of laughter. 'No, but it's not a secret. Leo had leukaemia as a teenager.'

'Oh, that's terrible.'

'Yes, it was.' Logan dragged a hand through his hair. 'But it was a long time ago. I rarely think about it now, but at the time...' His eyes took on a shadowed hue. 'It was pretty ugly. I took a leave of absence from school for a few months to be with him and basically ran amok, dodging the palace tutors and entertaining Leo as much as I could during his weaker moments.' He shook his head as if to clear the memory. 'You do not want to challenge me to a game of Monopoly,' he said. 'I'm an expert.'

Always having assumed that her boss was as cold-hearted as he was rumoured to be, she was moved to discover once again that, at least where his brother was concerned, he was anything but. 'I'll keep that in mind,' she said, her tone softening as she added, 'That was really nice of you...to stay with your brother, considering how you must have been feeling at the time.'

'It wasn't *nice*.' As if rejecting her sympathy, his voice turned hard. 'It was *necessary*. My parents were unavailable to give him the care that he required. Someone had to step up and I was glad to do it.'

'I understand completely.'

And she did. She'd stepped up many times since Peta had become pregnant and she wouldn't change a thing either.

Something passed between them as he looked at her. Some level of understanding that went deeper than anything they'd ever shared before.

'Do you think you should take a seat for landing?' she offered, unsure how to deal with the unexpected connection between them, as well as being aware that they were perilously close to landing.

Logan glanced out of the window and surprised her by resuming his seat again. When the plane lightly touched down on the tarmac Cassidy felt a whole new bundle of nerves jump around inside her stomach.

In a short time she would be meeting Logan's family and she'd never felt her small-town roots as keenly as she did right now.

'So when I greet your brother I curtsy and call him Your Majesty—is that right?'

'Yes.' He stood up and straightened his shirt cuffs. 'Though you needn't worry about mucking up your greeting. I think my brother has bigger issues to face.'

'I know. But I don't want to get it wrong.' The last thing she wanted to do was draw attention to herself. 'And I curtsy to your mother as well.'

'Yes. And since she was Queen she is still referred to as Your Majesty.'

'Okay,' Cassidy said, a look of concentration on her face.

Logan gave her a faint smile. 'It's not like you to be nervous. You weren't when you met me.'

'Of course I was nervous.' She shot him a quick look. 'It was a job interview and I really wanted the job.'

'You hid it well.'

'Another of my superpowers.'

He gave her a bemused smile. 'How many do you have?'

'Not many. I think that's the last one.'

He shook his head as if there was something about her he couldn't fathom, and placed his hand in the small of her back to indicate that she should precede him toward the doorway.

Flustered as much by the small gesture as the warmth of his hand, she barely registered when two imposing men in sharp black suits stepped into the plane. For a moment she thought they were being hijacked and then they nodded at Logan.

'Your Highness.' They greeted him in unison and Cassidy's eyes widened. Should she be calling him that now? 'The car is here.'

'Thank you.' Logan gestured for her to precede him and as soon as the bright sunlight blinded her she came to a dead stop. She hadn't realised he had followed so closely behind her until she felt his breath fan the nape of her neck when he spoke.

'What is it?'

'Just…the sun.'

Feeling gauche again, she sucked in a deep breath, her eyes following the cavalcade of black SUVs lined up on the tarmac like hyphens on a page. Aware that she hadn't moved and that Logan was waiting, she collected herself and descended the stairs as if she did this sort of thing every day of the week and twice on Sundays.

Cool, Cassidy, she reminded herself. *Remember to be cool and to not look like Dorothy straight out of Kansas at everything you see.*

Highly attuned to her boss's every movement as the cars headed off in formation, Cassidy saw Logan's jaw harden as he read an email on his phone.

'More problems?' she asked quietly.

'Yes,' he said. 'Leo won't be at the palace to meet us. He's taken his new woman into hiding to protect her from the media fallout. He's promised to call me later.' By the disdain in his voice Logan wasn't happy with that idea. 'A press release is already being prepared to confirm his abdication. The palace is in lockdown to contain the fallout from the media speculation.'

'That makes sense.' Cassidy pulled up the stock market app on her tablet. 'Arrantino banking stock has fallen by eleven percent in New York and while that's not catastrophic the reports suggest that the spillover will affect trading in many of the local businesses. On top of that—' she paused, knowing that he wouldn't like this next bit '—the Peterstone Organisation has pulled out of the Westgate deal.'

Logan swore roughly. 'Whoever leaked my brother's plans to the press is going to wish that they hadn't when I'm finished with them. But forget Peterstone. I suspect that they're overcapitalised as it is and the leadership crisis has given them the excuse they were looking for to pull out without losing face. Instead contact the Kellard Insurance trustees. They showed some interest in investing in the tunnel at one point and I know they're still looking for an equity stake to put their pension fund into. It might bridge the gap in time to make the tender deadline.'

Noting down everything he said, Cassidy looked up in time to see their car pass through a large stone archway that separated the countryside from the city of Trinia, Arrantino's major metropolitan and business centre.

'Wow, it's beautiful,' she murmured, her eyes glancing over a city that seemed to perfectly blend centuries-old buildings with brand-new constructions. 'And hardly any traffic. That's amazing for a city with just under a million citizens.'

Logan gave her an amused look. 'That's because the traffic has been cleared for our arrival. Once we're through, this boulevard will resemble Fifth Avenue at rush hour.'

'Oh, sorry.' She turned her attention back to the tablet, embarrassed.

Logan took her chin in his hand and turned her face so that she was looking at him once more. 'Why are you sorry?'

His fingers felt warm and strong and a liquid bubble felt like it burst deep inside her. 'I just keep making mistakes.'

'That wasn't a mistake. You don't know the royal protocol.'

'No.' Her throat felt thick and she swallowed, wanting to move and not wanting to move at the same time. 'It's just a little overwhelming, I suppose.'

Logan's brows arched. 'You'll be fine. This will be all over before you know it.'

Cassidy sucked in a soft, deep breath when Logan released his hold on her, her traitorous skin tingling from his touch. Within moments they were turning into the wrought-iron gates that led to the Royal Palace. The cars rumbled slowly over the wide cobblestoned drive that opened out into a massive forecourt.

'That's my great-grandfather, Javier,' Logan said, noticing her staring at a large statue of a military figure on a rearing horse as the cars stopped at the main entrance to the palace. 'He prevented the French from invading our humble country, thus aligning ourselves more closely with the Spanish, and becoming a national hero.'

'That would explain why Arrantinians speak a version of Spanish.'

'We were part of Spain for a long time before my great-great-grandfather seceded, so we go back a long way with our neighbour. That wasn't the easiest of battles either and you'll see his painting front and centre as you walk through the front doors.

'The palace is amazing. There must be a thousand windows on this side alone. I've seen pictures of it, of course, but in the flesh…'

'It's imposing. But it's meant to be that way. To put off any interlopers who thought we were fair game for a small kingdom, and to make any others envious of Arrantino's wealth.'

'Ah, the shock and awe trick.'

Her lips curved into a smile, but Logan obviously didn't share her humour because he turned away as a footman opened his door.

'Your Highness.'

She tried not to let his abrupt dismissal affect her by reminding herself that she was here to work, not to entertain him, but she wasn't completely successful.

He held his hand out to assist her from the car and Cassidy took it, even though she didn't want to. He gripped her fingers firmly, releasing her as soon as her feet touched the ground as if he felt the same tremor that she did when they touched. Which was probably the most fanciful thought she'd had yet and was evidence that maybe she wasn't as completely back to normal as she would like.

Something to work on.

Turning toward the stone steps, she was just in time to see Logan grin widely at the portly man in a suit and waistcoat standing to attention in front of him.

They greeted each other in Arrantinian before Logan turned back to her. 'This is my assistant, Cassidy Ryan. Cassidy, this is Gerome. He has been with our family for, what is it, Gerome? One century or two?'

'Sometimes it feels like two, Your Highness,' the retainer deadpanned.

He shared a look with Logan that seemed to suggest that right now it seemed like even more.

'Indeed.' Logan shook his head. 'Is my mother about?'

'Her Highness has a meeting with the director of the festival of the arts but she has been informed of your arrival. Housekeeping is preparing your apartments for your return and the King advised that you are to have free use of his offices.'

'Very good. Please arrange for a selection of pastries and extra-strong coffee to be delivered there.'

Now that they were here, Cassidy sensed the huge responsibility that truly faced her boss and she couldn't help feeling sorry for him. Her small problem of having to find another place to live seemed minute in comparison.

'Follow me,' Logan directed, striding through two huge wooden doors that stood about twenty feet tall.

They made their way towards the rear of the palace and Cassidy barely knew where to look as they passed through the vaulted, richly carpeted hallways lined with antique furniture and centuries-old artwork interspersed with oak-tree-thick marble pillars. The feeling was one of peace and serenity and if she hadn't been rushing to keep up with her boss she would have slowed her pace to fit the setting.

The King's formal offices were made up of four rooms, large and airy with French-style windows that overlooked emerald-green lawns bordering the river. The Arrantino mountain range majestically filled in the backdrop, the sky already a blinding azure blue.

The main office was uncluttered and contemporary, a large walnut desk taking up the centre position with comfortable cream sofas beneath French windows, and centuries-old paintings and modern bookcases lining the walls. This room alone was the size of her apartment back home and it was difficult not to gape.

'Do you want me to use the desk we passed on the way in?' she asked, her tablet in her hand as she prepared to stop gawping and get down to business.

'No. Set up on the sofa for now. I'm assuming Leo's private secretary uses that desk so I'll have another one brought in here temporarily.'

As soon as he spoke a slender woman with the grace of a dancer stepped into the office. With midnight-black hair, red lips and the build of a greyhound, she looked like she belonged on the set of a nineteen-fifties French film noir.

'Welcome, Your Highness.' Even her voice was smoky-soft with mystery. 'The King sends his apologies for not being here to greet you.'

'Margaux. It's good to see you again. This is Cassidy, my assistant. We'll need a desk brought in here. Can you arrange it?'

'Of course, sir. Is there anything else?'

'You don't happen to know the whereabouts of my brother, do you?'

'No. He didn't say.'

Logan's mouth pressed into a flat line. 'I'll want a debrief soon, but I'll let you know when.'

'As you wish. I'm at your disposal.'

Wondering just how much the other woman would be at his disposal, Cassidy caught the catty thought and banished it. Margaux had acted like a consummate professional—just as she needed to do—and she set her phone and laptop on the coffee table while she replied to a new email that had just come in requesting data on a deal they had not long closed.

Relieved to have work to focus on, she emptied her mind of everything else, only stopping to enjoy a delicious pastry and welcome cup of coffee from a team of servants who came and went as discreetly as mice.

An hour later an older woman who was sharply beautiful with styled blonde hair and timeless blue eyes a shade lighter than Logan's entered, almost breathing fire.

'Logan.' She didn't bother knocking as she swept into the room. 'It's good to see you. Leo said that he had brought you up to speed on the crisis.'

Logan bowed in greeting before kissing the woman on both cheeks. 'He's informed me of what he intends to do. I plan to change his mind about it. May I introduce you to Cassidy Ryan, my executive assistant.'

The woman cast Cassidy an appraising glance under which she felt like squirming.

'Cassidy, my mother, Her Majesty, Queen Valeria.'

His mother?

Shocked, Cassidy wobbled to her feet and lowered into what she hoped was a decent curtsy. 'Your Majesty, it's a pleasure to meet you. You have a lovely home.'

The Queen barely gave her a nod, dismissing her out of hand as she turned back to her son. 'Do you know where Leo has gone? He hasn't apprised me of his whereabouts.'

'Not specifically,' Logan said. 'Only that he's taking care of the woman he's currently seeing.'

His mother made a moue of distaste. 'That is so like Leo. He's such an emotional animal.' She shook her head as if that were a very bad thing. 'Don't think for a minute that you will be able to talk him out of his current plan of action. He's very set about abdicating. And so he should be, given the scandal.'

'You only think that because of the past.'

'I've forgotten the past,' she said briskly. 'As should you. The future is all that matters and our country needs you. You can't distance yourself from us for ever, and you will make a great king. You've always been level-headed in a crisis.'

'I don't want the role,' Logan ground out.

'Maybe not.' His mother eyed him, then continued, 'The new modern art wing at the national museum must be opened this afternoon, and then there is a meeting with the cabinet tomorrow. If Leo's not back, you'll need to attend that as well.'

'Isn't there someone else who can open the museum?'

'No. I have a choral exhibition to oversee. And the director of the museum will be expecting someone of senior rank since he's already been promised an audience with the King.'

'Fine. Just tell me that I'm not expected to make a speech.'

'Of course you are. And there's one more issue I need to table.' His mother gave him a pointed look. 'Your future intended.'

Logan shook his head and scowled at his mother. 'I

haven't agreed to take over yet,' he pointed out. 'And neither do I have an intended.'

'Which is why I've put together a list of potential candidates for you to consider.'

'Your Majesty.' Logan's voice was dangerously soft, his blue eyes piercing. 'Finding a wife is the lowest item on my list of priorities.'

'I know it is.' His mother arched a brow that suggested that she didn't care a whit what was on his list of priorities. 'Hence the need for someone to take charge in this regard. And before you regale me with your intention to find your own wife, may I remind you that you haven't found one so far and as the King-in-waiting you need to produce an heir. But this time we don't want any outsiders. You must choose someone from our echelon of society who knows exactly what is expected of one in royal life. The monarchy won't survive another mistake or another scandal.'

Logan gave a growl under his breath and ran his hand through his hair. '*If* I am to become King, I'm aware of what my future obligations will entail.'

'Good, then there won't be any issues about it. I'll have Margaux forward the list to your email.'

'I'm sure it will make riveting reading. Cassidy, can you liaise with Margaux to see if Leo had drafted a speech for this afternoon? I may as well start with something that *actually* needs my attention.'

'Of course.'

Cassidy curtsied again to his mother before quickly leaving the room. Frankly she couldn't get out of there fast enough. She was used to being the least important person in the room, but to his mother she had been all but invisible.

'I really don't think you should be calling your assistant by her first name,' she heard his mother say before she had fully closed the door behind her. 'It has a tendency to make them believe that they are closer to you than they really are.'

'Cassidy is my employee. That's all she has ever been and all she ever will be, and she knows that.'

'I hope you're right, Valeria replied. 'If she developed personal feelings for you she would have to go.'

'I'm well aware of that. If she developed feelings for me I'd want her to go.'

'Can I help you?'

Caught eavesdropping when she really hadn't meant to, Cassidy jumped. Margaux was watching her with open curiosity.

Logan's comment that she knew exactly what she was to him was a timely reminder that whatever she had been feeling up to now about her boss was completely one-sided. Which she already *knew*, but there was nothing like having something confirmed to really bring it home.

'The King's speech for the museum this afternoon.' She gave Margaux what she hoped was a confident smile. 'If you have one, can you please forward it to me as soon as possible?'

CHAPTER FIVE

AN HOUR LATER Cassidy had almost convinced herself that she was working out of her own New York office until Logan stopped beside the sofa and she glanced up and then around to see antique furniture and blue and gold flock-covered walls.

Logan's presence here seemed more imposing than ever. His handsome face was grim and Cassidy's belly did a mini-flip to find him standing so close to her.

Clearly his mood hadn't improved from earlier that morning and she once more found herself feeling sorry for him. He'd been fielding calls from New York since speaking to his mother, sorting out issues with the bank and acting as if it was business as usual when it was anything but. At least for her. This palace... his mother...the gravitas that permeated the air was a step up from even the bank's hallowed hallways. Not to mention the information that he was expected to marry someone from a noble family. The thought made her throat thicken because she had never considered that Logan would give up his bachelor lifestyle for anyone. He had always seemed so unattainable and she supposed he still was because although he might have to marry if he became King, it wouldn't be to an ordinary woman like her.

'No contact from Leo yet?'

His voice was calm, but she knew he was growing impatient.

'I'm afraid not.'

His mouth tightened as he rolled his shirtsleeves down over his muscular forearms and fastened his gold cufflinks. 'I've given him your number in case mine is busy and I don't care what I'm doing. If he calls, interrupt me.'

'I will.'

'How have you found Margaux?'

More sophisticated than she could ever hope to be.

'Great. She's very particular and thorough, and she's been very helpful. She forwarded your brother's speech and I've reworded some of the components to make it sound more like you. I sent it to your phone.'

'Then we're good to go.'

'We?' There was that word again and Cassidy pushed her glasses closer to her face with the tip of her little finger. She hadn't anticipated that Logan would want her to go with him on an official visit. He'd been handling royal affairs since he came out of nappies, whereas the most formal occasion Cassidy had attended was her niece's high school awards night.

'Yes. I want you there. I need an update on the Westgate tunnel deal.'

'Actually, I can give you that now.' She swallowed heavily. 'Kellard are definitely interested and I've arranged a tentative video conference with the trustees this Thursday. That way if it all comes off we'll still sign off on the tender bid by close of business that day. Everyone is on standby pending your approval.'

'And this is why I can't do without you.' He gave her a smile that made her breath catch. 'Of course I approve. We can set it up at the conference room down the hallway. You'll have to clear it with the IT depart—'

'Already done. I'm waiting for the head of IT to get back to me about it.'

Logan nodded. 'Let me know as soon as he does. In the meantime, pull the relevant information together and get any new figures from Accounting.' He glanced down at his phone, frowning. 'What are the Cliff Notes on this speech I'm expected to give?'

'The contemporary art movement in Arrantino and how it has influenced the direction of art on the world stage. There are also some awards to give out to the students who received grants last year.'

'Great. I know more about tropical fish than I do about contemporary art on any stage.'

Unprepared for his sudden display of humour, Cassidy barely kept a laugh from escaping her throat. The last thing she wanted was to find her boss funny, it would only make him more appealing when she was trying to find reasons for him to be less so. 'It sounds quite fascinating, actually. Apparently the light in Arrantino during the summertime would make Van Gogh weep.'

'You're an art buff?'

Cassidy instantly bristled at the implied surprise in

his voice. 'When you grow up in a small country town you become curious about everything.'

He cocked his head, studying her far too intently. 'It wasn't a criticism. Where you grow up doesn't define who you are as a person.'

Doesn't it?

Cassidy felt the knot of bitterness well up inside her at how easily the folk of her home town had judged her family as no-hopers after Peta's pregnancy, and then her own drastic miscalculation when she'd tried to win a boy's affection when she had agreed to send him a photo of herself in her underwear... Had she known he was going to share it with his friends...laugh about it...call her a...

She shook her head, the shame of knowing she had been as naïve as to think that one of the most popular boys at school had actually liked her for her still made her feel ill. She'd embarrassed herself and her father and the only good thing about it was that it had no bearing on her life now. No one else would ever have to know. Logan would never have to know.

Turning back to him, she reached for her handbag, feigning a lightness she didn't feel. 'Forget I said anything. Shall we go?'

Logan hesitated, seeming to see something in her expression that he wanted to explore, and Cassidy forced herself to remain poker-faced. It might be a new day but things had still yet to return to normal between them and she knew that was her fault entirely.

Logan frowned as Cassidy kept her attention firmly focused on her phone during the car ride to the museum.

Things had yet to return to normal between them and for that he blamed himself entirely. He was just too aware of her for comfort, his senses tuned into her in a way they never had been within the structure of his glass office.

He took in her neat hair and gabardine suit. Her low-heeled shoes. She looked the same as always and yet he couldn't get the picture of her wet and unkempt out of his mind. He couldn't shake the image of that see-through blouse, and during the short nap he'd caught on the plane he'd dreamt of peeling it from her body.

Knowing his sudden obsession with his EA was most likely due to the tension created by his brother's possible abdication didn't help. Neither was clamping down on the thoughts every time they arose. It was as if his body was running on a different track from his mind and for a man used to being in control of himself and everything around him it was concerning.

Deciding that dwelling on it wasn't going to help either, he turned his attention to the speech he needed to give, memorising the key aspects, and only glancing up when the car arrived in front of the museum. Built halfway through the last century, it was one of Arrantino's landmark tourist destinations due to the intricately placed mosaic tiles around the outside.

His great-grandfather had commissioned it. His father had added a wing. Now he was opening another one.

Following in the old man's footsteps?

Not if he could help it. And especially not with Cassidy, whose professionalism was the aspect of her nature he admired most. He'd never ruin that by giving in to his baser desires.

Cassidy lifted her head as if sensing the sudden shift in his mood.

She was good at that, sensing what he needed when he needed it.

The noise from the crowd clustered behind the barriers went wild as his door was opened. Cassidy's eyes widened and he gave her a look. 'Welcome to the other part of my world.'

She peered at the expectant crowd. 'I think every unattached female in Arrantino got the message that you would be here this afternoon.'

Amused by her observation but determined to close down any thoughts of that nature, Logan shook his head. 'Stick close and follow my cues.'

Stepping from the car, he reached back to offer Cassidy his hand before he could think better of it. Once again a tingle of unwanted awareness slid up his arm and his eyes cut to hers. Soft colour winged into her face as she snatched her hand back as if she too had been burned by the brief contact.

Frustrated that even the mildest of touches could set off alarm bells in his head, he was determined to not touch her again. Or ride in a car with her given that her floral scent was still clinging to him.

Intensely glad that the palace security team had kept the hungry paparazzi at bay, he greeted members of the public for five minutes before joining the museum director on the steps to the entrance and heading inside.

'It's an honour to have you here in His Majesty's

stead, Your Highness,' the director gushed. 'We hope the King is well.'

'The King is fine,' Logan said. 'You have a good turn-out today.'

'Thanks to your visit. The recipients of the royal grants are very much looking forward to meeting you.'

'And I them.'

Turning to ensure that Cassidy was okay, he turned to find her deep in conversation with various staff members, seemingly undaunted by the pomp and ceremony of the occasion.

As if sensing his eyes on her, she raised her head, giving him a questioning look he translated to mean, *Do you need me?*

Part of him instantly replied that, yes, he did need her, but since it wasn't a part of him that controlled logic and discipline he ignored it, giving a subtle shake of his head and tuning back into the director's descriptions of the innovations that had taken place in the museum since he'd last visited.

There was an air of gravitas to the whole affair and Logan wasn't sure if it was because his brother's potential abdication was overshadowing the situation or not, but try as he may he couldn't seem to get the young artists who were the recipients of the royal grants to relax and open up about their work with the freedom he would have liked.

Frustrated, he was digging deeper into the motivation of one particularly interesting piece of work when a soft laugh rang out in the quiet room.

Every head turned toward his Cassidy, who had her

fingers clamped over her mouth to stifle her mirth. The artist beside her could barely contain her own laughter, and the director of the museum frowned sternly.

But Logan couldn't help moving toward the pair to find out what had made her laugh.

'Want to share?'

'Oh, I'm sorry.' She bit down on her lower lip as she realised that she had an audience. 'It's nothing really. I was admiring Michael's oil painting of snails, only for him to confess that actually they're pastry scrolls.'

'It's a breakfast theme,' the young artist confirmed graciously, 'but you could eat snails for breakfast if you wished.'

'Not the ones in my garden,' Cassidy confessed, making everyone around her smile.

She peeked up at Logan through her long lashes as they moved on to the next piece. 'I'm going to let you take the lead on this one,' she murmured. 'I'm likely to offend someone if I do it.'

'I doubt you could offend a flea,' he observed, finding his gaze riveted to her lively expression.

If he had thought her smile had been stunning during his plane taking off, it was nothing compared to seeing her so open and warm with the people around her.

And her enthusiasm was infectious, relaxing everyone around her.

It was the icebreaker he had been looking for and it completely changed the mood of the tour, replacing the dry discourse over the various pieces into lively, friendly chatter. Logan followed it up with a speech promising more grants in the future and a private moment with the director.

He was wondering where Cassidy had disappeared to when one of the staff informed him that she had ducked into the ladies' room. When she didn't reappear after a few minutes, Logan checked his watch and excused himself to go and find her.

Following the directions to the nearest ladies', he rounded a corner and was nearly knocked over as Cassidy barrelled straight into him.

Instinctively he caught her to him. His body immediately registered the contact of soft, curvy woman, his response to her so primal and inappropriate it left him speechless.

The sweet scent of her hair product infiltrated his senses and he filled his lungs with it.

Cassidy's fingers automatically went to push her falling glasses back up her nose, the move flattening her soft breasts against the solid wall of his chest.

As if she too registered the experience, her wide, shocked eyes flew to his.

It was a shock he shared given the raw bolt of lust that was already turning him hard.

Gritting his teeth against the assault on his senses, he absently noticed that her mouth was mere inches from his and wondered what it was about her that pulled so forcefully at his self-control. It took everything in him not to bridge that gap and lower her to the floor.

'Easy,' he said as she stumbled, his hands clenching her slender hipbones, part of him aware that it would be so easy to slip his hands further around to cup her rounded bottom.

She was tiny compared to him, the top of her head barely reaching his chin. Without her heels she'd be even shorter and he'd have to bend to kiss her.

For a moment, she didn't move, her breathing as laboured as his.

And then one of the catering staff rounded the corner, her startled gasp at finding them standing so close together very telling.

Stepping back, Logan ran a hand through his hair.

Cassidy straightened her jacket.

They both looked as if they'd been caught with their hands in the candy jar and yet nothing had happened.

Nothing other than what had exploded inside his imagination.

'We need to get back,' he said, dismissing the incident as if it had never happened.

Still shaken at having found herself plastered up against her boss with her arms wrapped around his neck, Cassidy remained avidly glued to her phone all the way back to the palace.

Fortunately Logan seemed just as disinclined to engage her in conversation, which was good because if he looked at her she was afraid that he would be able to read the naked desire written on her face if he did.

It was embarrassing really, how badly she had wanted to kiss him. It was as if two years of working together professionally had dissolved into a murky puddle of lust, never to be found again.

Acting as if nothing had happened at all, and maybe for him it hadn't, Cassidy trailed him as he strode into the King's offices. Flicking his cuff, he checked his watch and frowned. 'It's getting late. Perhaps we should call it a night.'

It was getting late, but Cassidy was functioning on New York time and that, combined with her sleep on the plane, meant that she wasn't tired at all.

'I'm going to get a bit more done,' she said, taking a seat at the smaller desk that had been placed on one side of the room for her use while they had been gone. 'You wouldn't believe how many requests for information have been forwarded to me. I swear in this day and age of instant information overload no one can wait for anything.'

'One of the drawbacks,' Logan agreed wearily. 'Not that we have anything firm to report yet.'

She saw the tension in his shoulders and the tight skin around his eyes and her heart knocked against her chest in sympathy. She'd never quite seen him as human before, but there were glimpses of it, like now.

'I'll handle it,' she assured him. 'I want to touch base with some of our larger clients and I also need to get back to a couple of the Kellard trustees who would prefer to speak to you directly instead of reading the prospectus.'

Logan grunted. 'I need to meet with Housekeeping in my apartment. If Leo should call—'

'I know. Come and find you.' Cassidy waved him off, needing some time on her own. 'Will do.'

Logan frowned as he stopped beside her. 'Don't

wear yourself out. Your energy level will hit bottom at some point.

Sure that he was right, Cassidy let out a breath of relief as he left the room, feeling like a balloon that had been popped by a pin.

She caught a glimpse of herself in a mirror on the far wall, surprised to find that she still looked the same as she always did. Somehow she'd expected a crazy woman to be staring back at her with wild hair and bright eyes. Because she didn't feel the same. She felt more unbalanced now than yesterday. But that was because everything had changed, hadn't it?

Being here with Logan, knowing her life would be different when she returned… Was it any wonder she was feeling so out of sorts? This was normal. She just needed to compartmentalise—something she had always believed she was very good at due to her messy childhood—and stop reacting physically to her boss.

He hadn't wanted to kiss her back in the museum any more than he'd wanted to kiss her in his apartment the night before. He kissed supermodels and society princesses. He did not kiss ordinary girls from Ohio.

Pulling out her laptop, she sat down behind the new desk that had been set up with an ink blotter and stationery. Everything was fine. Everything was exactly as it should be.

Not sure how convinced she was of the truth of that, she was nonetheless relieved when a staff member knocked and entered the office, wheeling in a covered trolley with alluring silver-domed plates.

'Please tell me you have hot coffee in that jug?'

Cassidy said, her saliva glands already salivating at the thought.

'Yes, ma'am. And some sandwiches. His Highness thought you might require some refreshments.'

'His Highness is a god,' she said, without thinking.

The young girl gave her a shy smile. 'He is, ma'am, yes.'

Just for a moment Cassidy wondered what it would be like to be waited on hand and foot, and then recalled the moment Logan had stepped out of the car at the museum and the adoring crowd had surged excitedly against the barriers to get his attention.

It had been like something out of a Hollywood film.

Logan had waved and smiled and as soon as he'd neared the museum the small delegation of staff had subtly straightened, standing to attention, wide smiles on their faces in anticipation of meeting him. Cassidy had noticed that he often had that effect. Whenever he entered a room the atmosphere buzzed with palpable electricity, his self-assurance a cloak that caused everyone else to defer to him without even realising that they were doing it. His very presence commanded respect from those around him. But it was even more pronounced in Arrantino, where his importance was beyond question.

A little overawed, she had found herself standing straighter as well, but of course Logan didn't bat an eyelash, completely relaxed and at ease, and accepting the fawning attention with unquestioning self-confidence. And why wouldn't he? This was the life he had been born into. And no doubt the attention would be even more servile if he did become King.

She wondered if the attention had something to do with why he didn't want to become King and then reminded herself that she was not going to be curious about him. It only served to make her more aware of him as a man, instead of as her boss, and she was very afraid that if she continued down that road she'd never be able to get off it.

Turning to work to ground herself again in reality, she opened the first email. Now that most of the business world had learned that Logan was in Arrantino, and not at the helm of the bank as usual, she was inundated with frazzled clients demanding to know what was happening.

It was a diplomatic minefield and she relished the chance to navigate it because if there was one aspect of her life she was confident in it was her ability to do her job. Only she suddenly wondered how much longer she would have the job.

If Logan did become King he would no doubt want someone who was conversant with royal issues as his assistant. Someone like the lovely Margaux. Which meant that Cassidy would be out one place to live and one job. The thought landed like a sickening thud in her stomach. Not only would she be finding new accommodation, or a housemate, when she returned to New York, but she might be looking for new employment as well. For someone who saw change as akin to death, she couldn't think of anything worse. It was as if some unseen force had taken hold of her life and shaken it up as if she were living inside a snow globe.

Glad when a new email landed in her inbox, she opened it to find that it was the list of marriageable young women his mother had promised to have her aide send through. Well, if that wasn't enough to ground her in reality, nothing was.

Work, she reminded herself as she felt the weight of all the turmoil around her weighing her down once more. *You're here to work so get on with it*.

Forty-five minutes later her phone rang from an unknown number.

CHAPTER SIX

'GOOD AFTERNOON, MISS RYAN. It's Leo, Logan's brother. I can't seem to get hold of my brother and I only have a short window to speak with him. Do you happen to know where he is?'

'Yes, Your Majesty.' Cassidy tried not to feel overawed, the King's deep voice reminding her of Logan's. 'I believe he's in his apartment. If you wouldn't mind holding I'll take the phone to him.'

'Thank you.'

Pushing to her feet, Cassidy slid her heels back on and dashed out the door. Having no clue where to go, she approached a nearby footman and asked for directions.

'I'll take you there myself, ma'am. This way.'

Sensing the urgency permeating every cell of her body, the young footman didn't waste time, wending his way up a grand staircase and along a richly decorated hallway until they reached a set of ornate cream doors.

She fervently hoped that Logan hadn't gone anywhere else because she knew how important this call was to him and wondered why he hadn't picked up his own phone.

'This is it, ma'am, His Highness's apartment.'

'Thanks.'

Cassidy checked that the King was still on the phone and gave the young footman a grateful nod as she knocked on the door.

Smoothing back her hair, she waited for Logan to tell her to enter and when she didn't hear anything she tried the handle, suddenly nervous as the door clicked open.

Telling herself that there was nothing to be nervous about, she stepped inside, her eyes widening at the sheer opulence of the room.

It was so stately and handsome she half expected Elizabeth Bennet to come wandering out of one of the rooms at any moment.

Feeling a sense of *déjà vu* at having once again entered her boss's private sanctuary unannounced, she moved further into the apartment, fervently hoping that she wasn't going to be confronted by muscles glistening with sweat and vitality from an intense workout. Assuring herself that the same situation was as likely to happen as—

'Oh, my God!'

Cassidy's hand flew to her stalled heart as she came face to face with her boss in the middle of the parquetry hallway.

This time he wasn't wearing anything as bad as gym clothes. This time it was much worse because the only thing he was wearing was a towel tied low around his lean hips, his ripped torso and corrugated-iron abs so much more delicious than her imagination could have conjured up.

'Please, tell me that this is a bad dream,' she groaned, a liquid heat unfurling low in her pelvis as she stared at the sleek perfection of his hard body.

In the process of rubbing his hair dry with another towel, Logan came to a complete standstill and stared at her.

'It's not a dream, bad or otherwise. Is that for me?'

Incapable of coherent thought, Cassidy had no idea what he was talking about.

'The phone, Cassidy.' Logan's voice was dark and low. 'Is it for me?'

The phone? The phone?

Appalled, she remembered that she had the King on the line and held it out to him as if it were a baton she needed to pass on to the next competitor in a relay. 'Yes, yes, it's for you.' Her heart was racing like a runaway train as he prowled toward her. Plucking it out of her hand, he told her to wait for him before he disappeared back down the hallway.

Feeling like the survivor of a car crash, Cassidy didn't move for a good few minutes, not wanting to do anything that might bring him back.

Then she took a deep breath, absently noticing a tray of fresh glasses and a silver jug beaded with moisture.

Suddenly parched, she poured herself an icy drink and thought about rolling the glass across her sweaty forehead to cool herself down.

Fortunately, drinking it had the desired effect and

she felt her heart rate start to return to normal, only to sense Logan pad up behind her. Just her luck that his phone call would be so short.

She didn't turn to face him, pretty sure that if he was still wearing the towel she'd resign on the spot. Because how could she possibly go on working for him and not picture him naked every time she saw him?

'That was my brother.'

'I know.'

'I was in the shower when he tried my cell.'

Cassidy took a gulp of water. 'I kind of got that.'

Logan shifted behind her. 'Are you going to look at me or stand facing the wall for the rest of the night?'

Hearing the irritation in his voice, she slowly turned and automatically scanned his body for clothing. Fortunately he'd changed while he'd been speaking to the King, and was now dressed in a T-shirt and sweatpants as black as his mood.

'I'm really sorry for walking in on you like that,' she said softly. 'Had I known—'

'Forget it,' he dismissed. 'It's becoming a habit I'm getting used to.'

'Well, I'm not,' she squeaked indignantly. 'And I can assure you it will never happen again. I'm going to return your private key card as soon as we get back to New York because I'm never going into your personal space again unless you're with me, or not there at all.'

Logan raked a hand through his still wet hair. 'That's not something you'll have to worry about in the future because I'm not returning to New York.'

'Oh.'

Knowing exactly why that would be, and seeing the weight of it in the tense line of his shoulders, she watched as he stalked to a minibar between a set of shelves and poured himself a healthy dose of something amber. Probably Scotch.

'Want one?'

He held up his glass and Cassidy shook her head. In the office she knew what was expected of her. She knew her role. Now, without the separation of Logan's oak desk and surrounded by metres of glass, everything was different. She was different. And so was he.

She also knew that if Leo had given up the throne, Logan wouldn't be happy. He hadn't wanted his life to change, but he was too honourable not to step into his brother's place if that was truly required. After all, this was the man who had sat by his brother's bedside while he'd been sick as a teenager.

In an attempt to get them back on track, Cassidy tried to focus on work. 'I take it from that comment about not returning to New York that your talk with your brother didn't go so well.'

Logan barked out a laugh. 'That's a polite way of putting it.'

'What did he say?'

'He's enamoured of this woman. Elly Michaels. She's an archaeologist and as my brother is a keen artefact-collector they've been bonding over five-hundred-year-old ceramics since they met six months ago. Apparently she makes him smile even when she's not there.'

Logan said the last with a healthy degree of derision but it made Cassidy go soft inside. 'Oh, that is so sweet.'

Logan's brow rose in mockery. 'Sweet? To be at the mercy of your emotions? I took you as far too sensible to take that view.'

She was sensible now, but she hadn't always been. Neediness had made her stupid and she'd never forget the disappointment on her father's face when his good girl had gone bad. When he'd discovered she'd sent that photo. And she had vowed to never succumb to the feeling again.

But she couldn't deny that, when her guard was down, like now, she felt something akin to that with her boss. Having refused to view him as anything other than her boss for so long, she didn't know why she was finding it so hard to switch back to that now, but she was.

Cassidy grimaced. 'I usually am, but…to find someone special like that is very rare.'

'You don't have to convince me of that. I'd go so far as to say non-existent.'

And she supposed she could guess as to why that was if his father had cheated on his mother so often.

'But tell me,' he continued softly, almost challengingly, 'does Peter share your romantic outlook on life?'

'I don't know if I'd go so far as to call my outlook romantic,' she said carefully, knowing that maybe, possibly, if she gave free rein to her deepest desires, it might come close. 'But Peta is definitely that way inclined.'

Her sister had always loved the idea of being in love and even the twins' father bailing on her hadn't been able to squash that side of her nature completely. Hence Dan…

'Lucky you,' Logan drawled in a tone that, had he been any other man, she would have said was jealous. 'To find a man who matches you so well.'

'Man?' A frown formed between her eyes. Then realisation dawned. 'I think we might have our wires crossed somehow. Peta is my sister.'

'Your sister?' Logan looked at her as if she had sprouted an extra head. 'Then who the hell was the guy who kissed you in your doorway when I picked you up?'

'That was Dan. My sister's fiancé.' She shook her head. 'Seriously, we've talked about Peta's reaction to my coming here… How could you think that she was a…a what? A lover? A boyfriend? I haven't dated in years.'

'Easily.' The arrogant gleam was back in his eyes. 'You're a beautiful woman. Why wouldn't I believe you were seeing someone?'

He thought she was beautiful?

'Because we work so closely together,' she said, flustered by the unexpected compliment. 'And I know every woman you date because I have to inevitably buy them goodbye gifts.'

'Clearly I don't know half as much about you. Why haven't you dated for so long?'

'Because I haven't been asked.' She felt her face burn under his intense scrutiny. 'But even if I had, I'm not interested in dating anyone.'

Not at all enjoying having the focus on a part of

her life that was such a dismal failure, she mentally searched for a distraction. 'You know what I do when I'm upset?' she said with Mary Poppins–like enthusiasm. 'I do something physical.'

A cynical smile twisted his lips. 'What are you suggesting, Miss Ryan?'

Whenever he addressed her like that she thought of sex and it took a lot to remind herself that he wasn't thinking the same thing. Only this time he was. But that was because he was moody and looking for an argument. And she was directly in the firing line.

'Not that kind of outlet,' she managed. 'I meant exercise. For me that's taekwondo, but for you I know it's running.'

His eyes gleamed speculatively as he considered her. 'How good are you?'

Cassidy frowned. 'That wasn't an invitation to spar with you.'

'I didn't take it as one.' Dark lashes lowered to conceal the compelling blue of his eyes. 'That's why I'm issuing one of my own.'

'But you don't even practise taekwondo,' she said on a rushed breath, her mind frantically searching for some way she could get out of this diplomatically.

Unfortunately Logan had his juggernaut expression in place. 'I know karate. It should make for an interesting session.'

Cassidy shook her head. 'There's no way I can spar with you.'

'Afraid I'll hurt you?' he asked softly.

No, she was afraid she'd have to touch him, and she

had enough brain cells still working to understand a bad idea when she came across one. 'It wouldn't be appropriate.'

That arrogant gleam returned. 'Why not? We're not working right now. And even so... I don't care about what's appropriate. I care about doing something I want. And what I want is to find out what my EA is made of.'

If she had to answer that, she'd say jelly. 'This is not a good idea.'

'Duly noted.' Logan's grin turned wolfish. 'Now go and suit up.'

Her *sister*?

Logan was stunned. How had he got that so spectacularly wrong? And why did finding out that she didn't have a lover make him feel so much better than before? It wasn't as if he cared if Cassidy had someone special back home and, really, it changed nothing between them.

Even if he had the freedom to explore the sexual spark between them, he wouldn't. Not only did she work for him but she was the kind of woman who would inevitably want more from him. The kind he tried to stay away from.

Still, he was aware that on some level he was playing with fire by inviting her to spar with him. Especially when he saw her walking toward him in her white cotton dobok and matching black pants, her long hair pulled into a plait that trailed down the centre of her back like a silky horse's tail. She looked younger like this, her lovely face and clear eyes so guileless he could see just how nervous she felt.

And she probably had good reason to feel that way. He wasn't exactly himself right now.

Finding out that Leo would not reconsider his abdication, making him the next King of Arrantino, had shaken him. He still wasn't convinced that his brother giving up the throne for a woman was the wisest course of action, but he'd kept his own council this time. Leo had accused him of being over-protective in the past, but having sat by his brother's bedside while he'd gone through months of chemotherapy had been painful to watch. Then having his marriage fail… Was it really being over-protective to want to prevent someone you loved from experiencing pain?

Because what if this Elly woman turned out to be just another version of Anastasia?

Grabbing two bottles of water from the refrigerator, he joined Cassidy. She looked stiff and uncertain as she glanced up at him, her green eyes brighter without her glasses.

'You're not wearing your glasses?' he asked, not recalling a time he had seen her without them before.

'No. I generally need my glasses for work because I suffer from eye strain, but I don't need them all the time.'

Something else he hadn't known about her.

He led her downstairs to the gym and pushed open the door, wondering how many more secrets she had that he had yet to uncover.

Uncover?

He frowned. He didn't want to uncover Cassidy's secrets.

Her plait swished as she walked ahead of him beckoning him to wrap his fist around the thick length and tug on it until her mouth was under his. There was definitely one secret his body was keen to uncover but he forced his mind not to go there. She was out of bounds.

The gym wasn't empty. Two palace employees who looked to be in the middle of a workout were there, but Logan wasn't in the mood for company and levelled a look at them both.

Mumbling a formal greeting, both men collected their gear and left through the second door.

Cassidy turned to face him, her slender brow arched as she toed off the soft slippers provided for palace guests. 'You made them leave.'

'Yes.' He placed the two water bottles on the bench against the wall, completely unapologetic.

'You didn't have to do that,' she said. 'We're only going to be using the mat.'

Logan lifted a brow. 'Oh, did you want an audience when I soundly beat you, *Miss Ryan*?'

A soft blush touched her cheeks as she shook her head. 'I may look small, *Mr de Silva*, but I've beaten men larger than you before.'

Her beguiling gaze raked from his broad shoulders down over his powerful thighs and he actually felt a shiver move across his skin.

As if she had no idea of the effect she had on him, she gazed at him steadily from across the mat. Which was probably for the best.

Obviously feeling the swirl of his shifting emotions, she tilted her little chin up at him. 'So what happens now?'

Making the decision to switch his brain from sex to sparring, he toed off his runners and moved to stand in the middle of the mat. When he had offered to spar with her it had been out of a genuine need to let off some steam and, okay, a small amount of curiosity to see her in action. Knowing that she held a senior black belt had only elevated that interest. 'Now we spar,' he said.

Aware of every move she made, he noticed the moment she hesitated. 'Actually, I meant about you becoming King. What's the process?'

'A notice will go out tomorrow.' She stepped back from him and stretched from side to side, bending to touch her toes to warm up.

Logan told himself not to watch. 'The coronation will be on Friday.'

'Four days from now?' She straightened and rolled her slender shoulders. 'Why so soon?'

'To avoid any more fallout for Arrantino and to ensure that the focus is on the future. Not the past.'

'That makes sense.'

Having finished her stretches, she came to stand directly in front of him, her subtle scent reaching out to ensnare him. When he didn't immediately move, her eyes flickered to his warily. 'You know we can still change our mind about this.'

'Too late.' He overrode his sensual response and bowed to her. 'I'm already having fun.'

And he was. Seeing another side to Cassidy was far

more interesting than contemplating how incredibly his life was about to change.

'I'm still not used to seeing everyone bow and curtsy to you as they have been today,' she murmured. 'Does that mean I'm supposed to as well?'

'Only when you first see me in the day.'

'Oh, sorry. I forgot this morning.'

'Next time it will be ten lashes at dawn,' he promised, bending his knees to take up the traditional karate stance. 'Shall we?'

Her green eyes gleamed as she observed him and he knew that she was relishing the opportunity to spar with him as much as he was with her. A dark thrill raced through his body at the prospect that he might have met his match.

Cassidy took up a similar pose, tracking his expressions and movements with the confidence of a seasoned practitioner.

Logan breathed in through his nostrils, once more picking up the scent of flowers and musk.

Which was when she struck, moving her arms in a quick series of blocking moves before sweeping his legs out from under him.

She laughed as he lay sprawling at her feet, the sound light and musical. Not at all put out by her getting the jump on him, he leapt lithely to his feet.

'Like that, is it?' he drawled softly.

She laughed again, dancing away from him lightly.

'First rule of combat. Never underestimate your opponent,' she advised, clearly delighted in her small victory.

Feeling alive and invigorated, Logan pulled a few light moves on her, impressed with her technique and her agility. Not that he seriously thought he was at risk of being defeated when she was so light he could lift her up with one hand tied behind his back.

'How is it you know taekwondo?' he asked, as he blocked another lethal combination of moves.

'My father insisted that my sister and I take self-defence lessons when we were younger, and I became hooked.' She threw in a high kick that he dodged. 'They offered lessons at our local YMCA and I used it as a break from reading.'

'Bookworm, were you?'

He used the question to distract her, and it worked because she wasn't ready as he forced her back on the mat and rolled her over his arm and sent her to the floor.

Pink with exertion, she jumped gracefully to her feet, scowling at him. 'You deliberately distracted me. And, yes, I'm boring if that's what you were getting at.'

'Boring?' With that mouth, and those eyes? 'You're turning out to be the least boring woman I know.'

His comment was followed by a serious of twists and kicks that had him roll off to the side rather than find himself face planting on the mat. She arched a brow, a smug grin curving her lips. 'You won't get me with fake compliments.'

Fake?

'I don't do fake.'

She gave him an uncertain glance and he used the momentum of her being on the back foot to use a series of kicking moves that were a combination of two different forms of martial arts, taking her by surprise as she tumbled again.

'That was illegal,' she complained, facing him.

'No, it wasn't. I practise Krav Maga as well.'

Cassidy rolled her eyes. 'Naturally you would know the most aggressive forms of martial arts.'

'Of course.' Logan shrugged. *'Basic Prince Training.'*

'Really? I would have thought that basic prince training would involve how to be demanding and get what you want.'

Logan grinned at the playful dig. 'That's *Basic Prince Training Part Two.*'

Laughing, she threw in an illegal move of her own, but Logan was primed for it, flipping her onto her back and straddling her waist with his strong thighs.

They stared at each other, both panting hard. Logan wanted to lean down and take her soft mouth with his own and almost did, but she pushed him back and he rolled to his feet.

'Why don't you want to be King?'

Not sure if she was trying to distract him again, he dismissed her question. 'Too much responsibility.'

'Meaning that you don't want to talk about it.'

He should have known she was too smart not to see through his flippant answer. 'Correct. Water?'

She took the bottle he offered and twisted the top, guzzling down a healthy amount. 'It always seems so glamorous,' she mused. 'You live in a fancy palace, you have servants at your beck and call, you can go whereever you want, people want to meet you and be with you, and you get to raise awareness on important issues.'

Logan drank deeply from his own bottle. 'Apart from raising awareness on important issues, the reality is very different. It's a life that is rarely your own. You're at the mercy of the press waiting for you to step out of line, you attract people who are interested in power and diamonds and not necessarily in that order, and you have no privacy. You don't have any secrets. It's frustrating.'

Cassidy's brow shot up. 'You like having secrets?'

'No.' His teeth ground together. I like having a life that's not built on a house of cards.'

'Are you saying that yours was?'

Accustomed to being surrounded by people who devoured gossip about him, and usually knew more than they let on, Logan found himself wondering if she was being straight with him. He'd had every psychological game played on him by women trying to make their position in his life permanent that he immediately questioned her sincerity.

Was he really so jaded?

Because there was nothing in Cassidy's expressive green eyes to suggest that she was anything other than sincere.

'Behind many closed doors life is different from that which we present to the world,' Logan said. 'Mine was no different.'

In fact, when their doors were closed they'd lived a

powerless childhood filled with nasty, unspoken grievances between his parents.

'Did you want to talk about it?'

No, he didn't. But somehow her soft invitation drew something out of him. 'My father wasn't quite the man the history books make him out to be. Behind closed doors he had a constant string of affairs. It didn't matter if a woman was married, single, an acquaintance, or if she worked for him, the only prerequisite for him to sleep with her was that she be attractive.' He gave a snort of disgust.

'It was fortunate that cell phones with cameras weren't around during the height of his glory days or it would have been much worse. As it was, the press dined out on the rumours of his exploits for long enough to make my mother check into a Swiss rehab facility for three months. That was the year Leo was diagnosed with leukaemia and my father's response was to head to a hotel with five international strippers.'

'Oh, wow, that's…'

'Water under the bridge,' he said starkly, wondering what had possessed him to reveal so much to her. He stepped back, hoping the physical distance would sever the moment of intimacy that had developed between them.

'I can see now why you don't want to be King,' she said softly. 'Why you don't want to be likened to your father, but it doesn't always have to be that way.' The look she gave him was full of a sympathy he'd never needed. 'If you live congruent to your values and want something different you'll be perfectly placed to create it.' She gave him a faint smile. 'Didn't you say that we don't have to be defined by our past?'

Yes, he had said words to that effect and having them fed back to him made him realise that in this instance he might not practise what he preached. Since he wasn't given to sentimentalising any aspect of his life he had never given it much thought, and he didn't particularly want to now.

'It's poor form to throw a man's words back at him,' he growled. Particularly if those words made sense.

Putting his water bottle down, he came at her again.

She danced out of his way with grace and skill. 'If it's worth anything,' she parried, 'I agree with your mother. I think you'll make an amazing king.'

Logan's heart kicked hard behind his ribcage. Her words *did* mean something but he was unwilling to explore exactly what that was either.

'Are we here to spar or to talk?' he challenged.

He didn't give her a chance to respond, forcing her back off the mat with a series of manoeuvres he was careful to keep controlled and smooth.

Sensing that he was holding back, she ramped things up with a look of determination he couldn't help but revel in.

Logan fended off her jabs, deliberately flinching as her foot connected with his ribs.

Immediately contrite, she stopped. 'Oh, no, did I—?'

Taking full advantage of her caring nature, he flipped her so that she landed flat on her back with her delicate wrists pinned above her head, his thighs straddling her slender waist to lock her beneath him.

'I win,' he breathed. 'You're well and truly pinned now.'

Cassidy raised her hips beneath him, but that only served to have him press her more firmly into the mat, which was when their sparring session turned to something else entirely.

Both of them went still, Logan's eyes locked on her lips as he leaned over her, Cassidy's eyes dark and uncertain as she gazed back at him.

The demanding ache in his groin pushed at him to do what he had wanted to do since he'd seen her completely undone in his apartment. Take her and damn the consequences.

She moistened her lips with the tip of her tongue, her fingers flexing beneath his hold.

His body throbbed with a powerful hunger that fogged his brain, his fingers burning with the desire to grab the belt at her waist and yank her dobok open so that he could feast on her high firm breasts.

If she made one move, gave him the slightest indication that she wanted this as much as he did, he'd— he'd what? Kiss her? Forget that she was his employee? He'd returned to Arrantino to put out the fires created by his brother's scandal, not to create one of his own.

As if sensing the shift in his emotions, she blinked, tugging her hands out of his hold.

Logan let her take control, rolling onto his back, stunned to realise that for the first time in his life he was not as in control of his actions as he liked to think that he was. That he had actually been closer than ever before to setting aside every one of his principles and doing something he would have surely come to regret had he followed through on it. And the consequences would be catastrophic at this point. He was going to be King. Now, more than ever, he needed to reinforce his ironclad self-control—not lose it altogether!

'Yes, you win.'

Her husky agreement broke through the litany of self-recrimination inside his head and Logan glanced up at her, his breathing still uneven. He wasn't sure what he'd won exactly but whatever it was he hoped his sanity was attached.

CHAPTER SEVEN

'DAMN,' LOGAN MUTTERED as the medal he was pinning to his military uniform slipped for the third time. Knowing that he should have taken his brother's advice and used a valet on the morning of his coronation, he glanced in the mirror and realised that the row of medals symbolising various aspects of his new role as head of his kingdom were not in a straight line.

Exasperated, he stalked out of his room and into the living area, his gaze zeroing in on Cassidy, who was standing by the window.

She glanced up from her trusty tablet as he appeared, every hair on her head tightly tied back and her standard black suit obscuring the toned, feminine body he'd spent the last four days trying to forget.

Which shouldn't have been all that difficult given the volume of work he had needed to juggle as outgoing CEO of a major bank and incoming King, but it had still been a challenge.

Now, though, with the big event mere hours away he found his mind straying, and it took considerable effort to stop his mind from returning to their—in hind-sight—ill-thought-out martial arts session.

He stopped in front of her, his gaze scanning the neutral expression she wore, as if she'd wiped the memory of how much they had enjoyed themselves from her memory. Something he knew he should appreciate but for some reason didn't.

In fact, her professionalism only made him want to wrap his arm around her waist and flatten her against him to find out how long it would take for him to bring back that dazed look in her luminous green eyes.

Eyes there were once more hidden behind her tor-toiseshell glasses.

'Did you need something?' she asked as the silence lengthened between them.

Yes, you, his libido barked before he could prevent it.

Scowling, he pointed to his chest. 'These medals aren't straight.'

She frowned. 'It's the middle two that are out of place.'

'I know,' he said, arching a brow. 'That's why I'm here.'

She shook her head, biting into the flesh of her bottom lip as she placed her device on a nearby table. 'You'll have to undo your jacket so I can get my hand inside. Otherwise I might prick you.'

Logan felt every muscle in his body tighten as he slowly slid the brass buttons from their moorings, disconcerted when even this simple act felt sexually charged between them.

As if she felt the same current in the air that he did,

she refused to look up at him as she carefully slid her slender hand inside his jacket so that it lay against his heart.

Focused entirely on keeping his pulse at an even rhythm, he stared at the top of her glossy head, wishing he'd now done the job himself.

'Are you nervous about today?'

Her unexpected question went some way to lessening the tension between them and he eased out a breath. 'Not especially,' he answered honestly.

Since the last phone call with his brother he'd reconciled himself to what lay ahead and almost felt at peace with it.

Having shocked himself by opening up to Cassidy about his concerns, he felt more at home with the decision. She had been right to remind him that while he might not have chosen this life for himself, he could, in fact, make this role his own. Her observation had helped propel his mind out of the past, where he had been unaware it had been stuck, and into the future where it belonged.

He still wasn't convinced that Leo had done the right thing in giving up his role as monarch, but that wasn't his business any more. His brother had made his choice. Logan only hoped he was happy with it, and that one day the two of them could get back to experiencing the close bond they had once enjoyed.

Cassidy glanced up at him, a faint smile on her lips. 'I won't tell anyone if you are.'

Logan felt bemused by her response. 'I believe you

wouldn't. But as you pointed out, I was born to this life. And don't they say what you resist persists?'

Like this nagging attraction that knocked him for six every time he got close to her.

'I don't remember saying that you were born to it exactly.' She readjusted her glasses on her pert nose, and he noticed the pulse at the base of her neck hammering lightly against her creamy skin. 'But I'd be nervous.'

She bent and pinned the last medal in place. 'There.' She quickly withdrew her hand from inside his jacket and he wondered why control was such a difficult concept around her. 'All done.'

'Now this,' he said, holding out a royal blue sash. He knew he could put it on himself, but he found that he was unwilling to end this quietly intimate moment between them.

She took the sash, her throat bobbing as she swallowed. 'Where does it go?'

'Under the epaulette on my left shoulder.'

Stepping closer, she pushed up onto her toes to feed the silk fabric through the epaulette, her breasts brushing his chest as she reached around his waist to grab it.

Logan's breath hissed out through his teeth and Cassidy's face flamed as she quickly secured it by his right hip and stepped back.

'Anything else?' Her tone was harried, as if she couldn't wait to get away from him.

'Yes. Are you coming tonight?'

'To the ball?' Her eyes widened. 'I didn't know I was invited.'

She hadn't been but he wanted her there and he

wasn't in the mood to question that sudden decision. 'You are.'

A frown pleated her smooth brow. 'Do employees usually go?'

'No.'

'Then I shouldn't.'

'You should. You've been instrumental in pulling everything together over the last few days. If nothing else, you deserve a night off.'

'Yes.' She grimaced. 'But I was thinking more along the lines of a warm bath and an early night.'

She moved away from him to pick up her handbag.

'You can have a bath any time.' He scowled, frustrated that she was clearly unimpressed by a gesture that felt more right the more he thought about it. 'If you're not there I'll come and get you.'

She shook her head, her expression still slightly harried. 'Can we discuss it later?'

'No.' Logan moved to her side. 'We'll discuss it now.'

'Fine.' She let out a rushed breath. 'I'll come.'

When her eyes flicked around the room, Logan stilled, his nostrils flaring. 'Did you just try to manage me?'

'Yes. No. Maybe.' Her hands fluttered between them. 'You have more important things to think about right now than whether I go to the ball or not.'

A noise from the doorway startled them both.

His mother strode in, her glance going between the two of them with barely suppressed censure. 'I agree with Miss Ryan. You *do* have more important things to think about.'

Cassidy made a quick curtsy but Logan barely suppressed a scowl at the intrusion. 'I disagree. I think Cassidy should attend the coronation ball.'

'Indeed.' His mother's raised brow spoke volumes. 'Well, that is a surprise.'

'Not really.' Logan redid the buttons on his jacket. 'Cassidy has worked by my side for a long time. I want her there.'

'It would hardly be fair to put Miss Ryan in a position that made her feel uncomfortable.' His mother's smile did not reach her eyes. 'Which reminds me, did you receive the list of potential marriage partners I forwarded yesterday?'

'Yes.' In the absence of being able to pour himself a drink at such an early hour, Logan moved to the side table and downed a short black coffee instead. Finding it cold, he grimaced. 'I've had a look at it, but, as I said when I first arrived, marriage isn't high on my priority list.'

'Once today is over, you can bump it up,' his mother said imperiously. 'And in the meantime five of the young ladies on the list will be in attendance at the ball tonight and I expect you to be at your charming best. These women have impeccable pedigrees and no damaging skeletons in their closets.'

Logan watched Cassidy fossick in her handbag as if she was looking for a way to dig herself out of the room. If she found one, he'd join her. Because there was no way he was ready for marriage and he wouldn't be pressured into it the way his parents had pressured Leo with Anastasia.

Sighing, he gave his mother his full attention. 'I won't let you down. But I need to do this my way.'

'I know. I am merely trying to ease your load.' Her gaze softened on his and she squeezed his arm. 'And when this is all done I'm looking forward to walking with you in the garden like old times. For now, I'll see you downstairs a little later.'

Without glancing at Cassidy, she left the room, leaving a cloud of perfume in her wake.

Cassidy glanced across at him, pushing her glasses up onto her nose, and he knew instantly that she wasn't going to accept his invitation to the ball.

'Don't even think about not attending tonight,' he said before she had opened her mouth.

'I don't think it's a good idea and neither does your mother.'

'My mother has just turned my coronation into a matchmaking event. Who else will bail me out when I need it?'

Cassidy gave him a look. 'You hardly need me by your side to keep a woman at bay. And you should use this as an opportunity to get to know whomever she's invited.'

Frustrated that she was being so stubborn, he glowered at her. 'I don't care about the women on the list.'

'You should.' Her tongue swept out to moisten her lips. 'They're all quite lovely. And very accomplished.'

'Stop echoing my mother's sentiments and stop defying me.'

He did not want to get to know the women on his mother's list. He wanted to get to know Cassidy. A thought that should have sent more shock waves through him than it did.

Her eyes widened as she looked at him. 'Your mother already doesn't like me. If I go tonight she'll like me even less.'

'My mother doesn't know you and has a deep distrust of staff members.'

Her brows drew down with concern. 'Because of your father's affairs?'

'Yes. She's really quite warm when she lowers her guard.'

'Maybe, but I—'

'Should be there tonight.' Logan stepped into her personal space, cutting off her protest. 'Despite what my mother said, it will be fun.'

He didn't want to question further why he wanted her there.

She gave him a baleful look. 'Even if I wanted to attend, I don't have anything suitable to wear.'

'I'll have a gown delivered here by the end of the day.'

'I don't want you buying me clothing.'

Which is what makes you so different from every other woman I've ever come across.

'Do it anyway.'

She sighed. 'You have your juggernaut expression on again.'

'My what?'

She shook her head. 'It's a look you get when you're not prepared to take no for an answer.'

Logan grinned at her slowly. 'Finally we understand each other.'

Cassidy stared at the couture gown hanging on the outside of her wardrobe door. It was a strapless design in mint green covered in a swirl of tiny crystal beads that looked like it would hug every one of her curves before flaring out at her hips to fall gracefully to the floor.

And there was no way she could wear it.

Her phone rang, and she knew who it was without checking the screen. 'I'm not wearing it.'

'You absolutely are wearing it,' her sister replied vehemently. 'It's stunning. And the twins and I want photos of you in it.'

Cassidy rolled her eyes. She'd been on the phone to her sister, talking about Logan's coronation, when the beautiful gown had been delivered and her sister had demanded she send a photo. And not only the gown had arrived but also accessories, and various bags containing an array of casual clothes, nightwear and shoes. How Logan had guessed her size she didn't know, but after having a quick look he'd got it exactly right.

Turning away from the shopping bags, she flopped back onto the bed. The coronation had been long and sombre, the full import of what Logan had now become slowly sinking in over the course of the day. 'I'm not wearing it because I'm not going.'

And surely Logan wouldn't come looking for her.

Not with two hundred important guests all queuing to pay homage to the new King.

'What do you mean?' Her sister sounded like she was doing the dishes as she chatted to her. 'Of course you're going.'

'I'm not. How did the exams go this week?'

'I think I did okay. I might have written down the wrong chemical compound for a face peel but I'm sure I passed. And don't change the subject. Why aren't you going?'

Because she had a bad, sneaking, *horrible* suspicion that she was falling for her boss. Just as her sister had warned her not to do.

And really she'd like to blame Peta for putting the thought into her head, but she was too honest with herself for that. The fact was she'd held a faintly burning candle for Logan since the day she'd started working for him. Spending time with him in Arrantino and really getting to know him, she'd come to learn that he wasn't the spoiled, arrogant, uncaring man she had convinced herself that he was.

He cared. Deeply. About his family. His country. It was love that he wasn't interested in and for all her spouting on about not wanting to find someone special for herself, she realised that she did. She did want someone in her life who looked at her the way Dan looked at Peta. She wanted someone to curl up next to at night. Someone who found her interesting and sexy and desirable.

And even though Logan would never be that man, her senses still leapt with excitement whenever he was near, her body switching to high alert in case he touched her again. Hoping that he *would* touch her again.

The other evening when they had been sparring and he'd braced himself over her in a display of masculine strength she had been so aroused, so feverish with need, she hadn't been able to move. All she had wanted was to reach up and pull his mouth down to hers.

Then he'd frowned, as if he'd read every one of her illicit desires and rejected them outright, and she'd managed to push him away. After that she'd gone into lockdown. Using her superpower to hide how she felt from him.

'Cassidy?' Her sister clanged a pot on the stove and cut into her uncomfortable ruminations. 'Why aren't you going?'

Not ready to admit to her sister how right she had been about everything, Cassidy sighed. 'I'm tired. It's been a long day.'

'Oh, fiddle,' Peta said. 'It's not as if invitations like this drop out of the sky every day. Of course you should go.'

'I thought you advised me not to get too close to my boss.'

'Oh, I might have been a bit cranky after you told me you wouldn't be home this week. No, Amber, do not open those cookies, dinner will be ready in a minute.' Peta let out a frustrated growl. 'Sorry, what was I saying? Oh, yeah. I shouldn't have taken my bad mood out on you. But I still hold to what I said. Do not fall for your boss. That would be a disaster. But you definitely have to go to the ball. Your boss has just been crowned King. This is a once-in-a-lifetime situation. You'll be like Cinderella. Who knows, you might inspire lust in someone who turns out to be Prince Charming. You are in a palace after all.'

'I'm not exactly lust-inducing material,' Cassidy said glumly, wondering if the lust Logan had inspired in her on that mat the other night had been at all reciprocated.

'That's only because of what happened with that jerk in high school,' Peta advised softly. 'But that was years ago. You're older now. And you're gorgeous.'

'You might think that but—'

'You *are* gorgeous,' Peta interrupted vehemently. 'But you don't see it. You need to stop hiding yourself away and let yourself shine. And don't pull that face I know you're pulling. You're just afraid to put yourself out there in case you get your heart broken. Well, guess what, kiddo? It might happen. But it might not. And despite what Dad told us, not all men are bastards. I finally found a good one.'

'So things are good with Dan?' Cassidy asked, glad for the chance to redirect her sister's energies toward her new fiancé.

'Fantastic. Now do me a favour. Have a shower, straighten your hair and fully immerse yourself in this opportunity so that you have no regrets.'

Cassidy stared at the ornate ceiling above her head. She knew her sister was trying to be helpful but it wasn't just the jerk from high school that had made her reticent to put herself on the line where relationships were concerned. She just didn't know whom to trust.

After her mother had left, and then the guy in college who had only wanted her for her study notes, on top of Peta now moving on…it just seemed that she was destined to be alone. And the only reason she had so few regrets in life was because of caution—not immersion.

Sometimes she wished that she could be more like her sister. Sometimes she wished that she had more faith in herself and a more positive outlook on life, but the thought of being wrong, of being caught unawares was too scary for her to take that view of life.

'When will you get to experience something like this again?' Peta coaxed.

Probably never, if she was being honest. 'I'll think about it. Say hi to the girls for me. I miss you all.'

'We miss you too. In the meantime, be like Alice and make lots of amazing memories tonight.'

'I thought I was Cinderella?'

Peta laughed. 'Be whoever you want. Be yourself. Create your own fairytale.'

'You've read too many fairytales to the twins. Life rarely works out that way. You know that.'

'Yes, but rarely is not never. You can make your dreams come true, Cass, you just have to want them badly enough. This is a once-in-a-lifetime opportunity. And don't forget, send photos.'

Her sister rang off and Cassidy pushed herself into a sitting position. She stared at the beautiful dress that was hanging so serenely on the hanger as if daring her to put it on.

She wondered if Logan had chosen it himself and then berated herself for the fanciful thought. As if he would have had the time, or inclination, to *choose* a dress for her. Likely he had called someone and delegated the task. That's what a sensible person would have done. That's what *she* would have done.

Because deep down she was a sensible person. Sensible and cautious. She thought of her father's voice after her sister had fallen pregnant, wearily telling her that he was just glad he had one level-headed child.

And apart from her one faux pas she had been level-headed. Level-headed and sensible. And a sensible person did not dress up in a gown they couldn't afford and attend a ball they had no right to attend.

But sensible people could also miss out on fun if they didn't take a chance now and then, a rogue voice inside her head taunted.

And she was older now. Wiser. Perhaps it was time to be more proactive in her life rather than reactive.

And perhaps the place to start with that was her job. With Logan now the King, his life was in Arrantino. Hers was in the States. And even if that wasn't the case, it wasn't as if she could work for him for ever. Not with the way she felt about him. Because something had shifted between them this last week and she couldn't seem to shift it back. Just being in the same room with him made her want to touch him and if he should ever guess how she felt she'd die of mortification.

But she didn't have to think about that right now, did she? She had time up her sleeve. Unless Logan wanted it otherwise, she could give it a month. Help him transition into his new role and put some feelers out to recruitment agencies in New York. In the meantime, she'd keep her head down, do her best to get on top of this pesky attraction and think about what she wanted for herself for a change.

Feeling marginally better now that she had a way forward, she found her gaze returning to the designer gown on her cupboard. As if pulled by a magical thread, she pushed herself off the bed and ran her fingers lightly over the gorgeous fabric. The silky material slid through her fingertips like a shimmering waterfall, the crystal beads catching the overhead light and glowing like tiny diamonds.

Once in a lifetime...

She took the dress down and held it in front of her, gazing at herself in the full-length mirror. She couldn't do it. She couldn't attend a royal ball as if she might actually belong there.

So don't think that. Go as a chance to see how the other half live and create some amazing memories. If you're already planning to resign, what's the harm?

Frowning as the rogue voice tempted her once more, she shook her head. Could she really wear a dress like this? It was a dress that belonged to a princess and, no matter how hard she dreamed, Cassidy knew that she would never be princess material.

CHAPTER EIGHT

AFTER WHAT FELT like the longest day in his life Logan would have liked nothing more than to loosen his tie and sprawl on the nearby sofa, maybe stream a rugby game and open a chilled bottle of ale—but that moment was a long way off. First there was dinner for two hundred followed by the ball.

He searched the large drawing room, which was rapidly filling with elegantly attired guests, for Cassidy, wondering if she would show up. He knew the gown he'd chosen on the drive over to Government House for the official handover had arrived because the stylist had sent him confirmation and photos.

Cassidy had been adamant that she hadn't wanted to wear it and she was probably the first woman to ever turn down a gift from him. In his experience his female companions adored receiving trinkets and the more expensive the better. Not that Cassidy was one of his *companions*, but she would look sensational in the green silk. As she would in the matching bra and panties—

You aren't going there, he reminded himself. He had

ordered the underwear on the advice of the stylist, not because he particularly wanted to see her in tiny scraps of lace and nothing else.

And if he believed that, he'd believe the moon was made of cheese...

Irritated with his one-track mind, he turned his attention back to his diplomatic advisor's assessment of a recent European summit and what it meant for Arrantino.

He knew he should be concentrating as come Monday morning it would be his job to make decisions on the laws that would serve Arrantino in the future but he couldn't focus.

What would he do if Cassidy decided that not only wasn't she prepared to wear the dress he'd chosen but that she wouldn't attend the ball at all? It wasn't as if she *had* to attend. The only work he would be doing tonight would be to thank his supporters and well-wishers.

Cassidy's official duties had ended when the coronation had come to a close. Since she'd worked above and beyond what was expected of her since arriving in Arrantino, he couldn't blame her for wanting to kick back and put her feet up. But he didn't want her to do that. He wanted her here, with him, and as much as that didn't make sense, denying it would only be lying to himself.

Never before had he had so much trouble keeping a woman to the role he'd predetermined that she would play in his life and it was starting to seriously bother him. Would he be able to work with her as his private secretary in the future? He hadn't mentioned the future role since their sparring session but it made sense for her to continue to work for him. They made an exceptional team. She knew what he needed sometimes before he knew it himself, and she had never been afraid to give her opinion, even if it didn't align with his. He'd come to appreciate that as much as her efficiency in running his office.

But would she want that? Would she want to move to Arrantino? He hoped so. She would be an asset to any company, and if there was one thing he prided himself on, it was that he was an astute businessman.

'Wouldn't you agree, Your Majesty?'

Having only half listened so far, he forced his mind to the current conversation regarding the latest round of trade talks Arrantino had entered into with India, one of their biggest export markets, breathing a sigh of relief when Leo appeared and politely dragged him out onto the terrace.

Swapping his champagne flute for a beer, Leo leaned against the balustrade and raised his own bottle in a toast. 'I thought I'd save you from having to listen to Joaquín pontificating about his exemplary knowledge of world affairs. You'll hear it over and over anyway.'

'Great,' Logan said sardonically, taking a grateful swig of the ice-cold beer. 'There's only so much sucking up a man can take in one day. I don't know how you did it.'

'Patience,' Leo said.

Logan raised a brow. 'Great. Then I'm stuffed.'

Leo chuckled, and slapped him on the shoulder. 'You'll be fine and you know it.'

'Maybe.' Logan knew he would still hate the goldfish-bowl aspect of the role, but the opportunity to address many of the challenging issues facing the world was something he was looking forward to sinking his teeth into.

'How are you holding up?' He gave Leo an astute look, knowing that with everything that had gone on, he couldn't be having an easy time of it.

'Mixed emotions.' Leo grimaced. 'I'm taking Elly and Skylar to Greece on Sunday. There's a dig taking place on one of the islands she's interested in and I thought it would be good to get away. The press haven't let up and she's worried about the impact it might have on Skylar.'

'I'm sure she is.' Logan's cynical heart thumped. He hated the thought that his brother was being taken advantage of yet again. It wasn't anything tangible. But it had happened before with Anastasia, and Leo's more trusting nature meant that it was possible for that to happen again. 'I just hope she's on the up and up.'

'Don't go there,' Leo warned, his chest expanding. 'I know you're just being protective, which is why I haven't bloodied your nose already.'

'I hope you're right.'

'I am,' Leo said. 'Elly isn't like Anastasia but, regardless, you really need to stop judging women from the jaded view that they're only out for all they can get.'

'I don't.' Logan gave a mocking grin at his brother's arched brow. 'Okay, perhaps I do. It's a habit that's stood me well so far.'

'Perhaps. But it also means that you look for the worst in people.'

He shrugged. 'It works for me. But, okay, I'll reserve my *jaded view* for when I meet her.'

He glanced over Leo's shoulder for any sign of Cassidy inside.

'Good. Because Elly asked me to extend an invitation to lunch tomorrow. I know from experience that it will be a low-key day so it shouldn't be a prob—' Leo frowned. 'That's the third time you've checked out the room inside. Who are you looking for?'

'Cassidy.'

Leo raised a brow. 'You invited her to the ball?'

'Yes, and I need you to take care of her tonight. Escort her in and make sure she's okay. And don't look at me like that. She's the best assistant I've ever had.'

Rather than lose the raised eyebrow, it went even higher. 'Are you sure that's all she is?'

Logan scowled. 'Now it's my turn to tell you not to go there. I'm not like the old man. I would never use my position to sleep with an employee.'

'Fine, fine.' Leo raised his hands in surrender. 'I know you wouldn't do that. I just couldn't help but notice you looked at her a lot today. And she seems nice. It wouldn't be the worst thing in the world for you to deviate from your usual type and choose someone real.'

'Other than the fact that she works for me.'

'Lots of successful relationships start out as working ones. That doesn't make them wrong. And it doesn't make you like our father, who used his position as a power play.'

'Regardless, the only thing Cassidy and I have between us is a close professional relationship.'

So why was his heart beating hard at the thought that she wouldn't turn up tonight?

'Your Majesty, my lords and ladies.' Gerome appeared just inside the open terraced doors. 'Dinner is about to be served.'

As soon as Logan stepped inside his eyes found Cassidy in the crowded room and two things became immediately apparent.

First, that she was wearing the gown and she looked every bit as incredible as he had known she would and, second, he would need to be on his guard if he intended to keep to his word and ensure that things remained completely professional between them tonight.

Cassidy's heart hammered inside her chest, her breath locked in her throat, as her eyes fastened on Logan.

Now the idea of seeing how the other half lived and creating new memories that had propelled her into the gown and then downstairs seemed like an unnecessary risk as he cut a determined path through the crowd towards her. He had changed out of his military uniform and into a sleekly cut tuxedo and bow-tie, his layered hair swept back from his rakish features, his vivid blue eyes narrowed with irritation.

'You're late,' he wasted no time in telling her. 'Which is unlike you. I thought I was going to have to send out a search party.'

His earlier threat that he would be the one to come and find her if she didn't show up hung in the air between them.

'Sorry…Your Majesty.' She half dipped, half curtsied in the tight-fitting gown, hiding her disappointment that he had not commented on how she looked, only now realising how much she had wanted his approval when he didn't give it.

Hating the needy feeling that balled in her stomach like cooling lava, she called herself a fool and thought seriously about turning around and returning to her room.

As if sensing her desire to escape, Logan latched onto her arm. 'You only need to curtsy to me the first time you see me.'

Feeling like she couldn't get anything right, Cassidy's throat constricted. 'This is the first time I've seen you tonight.'

'Just…' He looked like he was grinding his teeth. 'You've left your glasses off again.'

Seriously, he was going to talk about her glasses? 'I already told you that I don't need them all the time. And they hardly go with the dress.'

'I like your glasses,' he said gruffly.

Suddenly aware that he was standing so close that she could scent his cologne, she shook her head, her newly straightened hair swishing around her shoulders. All she could think about was how handsome he was and the only nice thing he could say was that he liked her glasses.

Unable to come up with a single response to that,

she glanced over his shoulder at the sound of a man clearing his throat. She'd been so overwhelmed at seeing Logan, not to mention the low-level hum of excitement in the room, that she hadn't even realised that his brother was standing right behind him.

'I think your glasses are very nice as well,' Leo said, casting his brother a reproving glance. 'And may I add that you look incredibly elegant this evening.'

'Thank you.' Cassidy gave him a grateful smile, which seemed to irritate Logan even more.

'I've asked Leo to escort you to the dining room this evening,' he said curtly. 'After that everyone will gather in the ballroom for the remainder of the evening.'

Fully aware of the schedule as she'd helped produce it, she nodded and made a mental note to never listen to her sister's advice again.

Nodding, as if he was pleased to have done his duty to her, he turned and strode toward the front of the room where his mother stood in a small circle of guests.

'Well…' Leo stepped forward and offered her his arm. 'That was interesting.'

More like horrible, Cassidy thought grimly. 'Actually, I'm not all that hungry.' She cast a glance toward the door she'd just come through as if to make sure it was still there. 'I might see if I can't get a snack delivered to my room. I'm sure no one will notice if I don't go through.'

'Oh, someone will notice,' Leo said with a broad grin. 'I think you're going to have to soldier on and do it now.'

Sighing heavily, Cassidy placed her hand in the

crook of his elbow and let him lead her past the milling guests, who watched them curiously as they headed toward the front of the line.

Feeling herself panic at all the attention, Cassidy tugged on the former King's arm. 'Really… I'm happy to stay at the back of the line.'

Leo gave her an amused glance. 'You might be, but protocol dictates that I can't. I'm obliged to follow my brother to the table and as his special guest you're obliged to stay with me.'

'Oh, I'm not his special guest. I shouldn't even be here.'

'Probably not. But you are so my advice is to relax and enjoy it.'

Cassidy pulled a face. 'Any advice on *how* to do that when so many people are looking at me as if I've just landed from another planet?'

'When in doubt just smile and nod. It's always got me through when I've had to work a tough crowd.'

Hoping that this crowd wasn't going to be any tougher to handle than her boss, Cassidy decided that now that she was here, wearing a dress that probably cost at least her monthly rental bill back in New York, she may as well make the best of it. At least until she could slip away unnoticed and collapse into bed with a film.

The line moved sedately toward the dining room like a procession of tourists lined up to get into The Met on a hot summer day, only much better dressed.

The cavernous dining room was dominated by three rows of glittering chandeliers and two long tables set with white tablecloths and gleaming silverware. Footmen stood to attention every few metres along the wall and Cassidy forced herself to concentrate on not tripping up in her new sky-high stilettos the exact colour of the dress.

Stopping beside Leo, Cassidy followed his lead and stood behind her chair, surprised when she looked up to find Logan directly opposite her.

When their gazes collided she felt all the air leave her lungs and suddenly she was back on the mat with him leaning over her, and she had a breathless feeling he was having the same thought.

Fortunately Leo murmured for her to take her seat, breaking the connection between them, and Cassidy let out a breath, telling herself that she had imagined the whole moment.

After that the dinner went surprisingly well. Leo was great company and the never-ending relay of mouth-watering dishes left little else to do besides eat and drink.

Of course she was conscious of Logan across from her the whole time, but fortunately he didn't scowl at her as she imagined that he might after his terse greeting. Instead, his testy mood seemed to have evaporated as he conversed with the guests on either side of him. Which didn't lessen her awareness of him, but it did mean that she could begin to relax and take in the splendour of her surroundings.

When the meal was concluded, Leo directed her to the ballroom, the largest room in the palace, with rich, red-flock-covered walls and gilt-edged thirty-foot-high ceilings with cherubs holding bows and arrows chasing each other across puffy white clouds.

Orchestra music drifted through the dazzling room that was bright and airy with the wall of French doors opened to take advantage of the balmy evening. Fairy lights twinkled like stars from the manicured gardens, beckoning guests to enjoy the stone terrace and tranquil surrounds.

Cassidy caught sight of Logan at the far end of the room, surrounded by a group of glittering guests. Wondering how many of those were the single women on his mother's list, she reminded herself that she wasn't going to think about that and turned to watch the crowd that had already taken to the dance floor.

'Shall we?'

Flushed with exceptional wine and food, Cassidy pushed all thoughts of Logan and his mercurial moods to the back of her mind and took Leo's hand. 'Yes, please.'

After that the evening seemed to fly by. Cassidy felt as if she danced with every man at the ball. But it was either dance or feel out of place in the crowd of people that, after their initial surprise at finding that she worked for the new King, subtly dismissed her when they realised that she didn't have a title preceding her name. Just as his mother had implied that it would.

To be fair, some of the guests were nice. Like the Italian twin countesses with whom she had passed a pleasant half-hour talking about the tricks identical twins played as children. But it had soon became apparent just how different their lives were when they'd mentioned their summers spent in Portofino and shopping trips to Milan and Dubai. Cassidy hadn't thought that taking her nieces on the subway to Coney Island and getting to the sales early at Macy's quite cut it, and it had been a relief to accept the hand of the next man who had asked her to dance.

And it had taken her mind off the number of suitable women Logan had been dancing with all evening. A statistic she'd like to not have in her head, but which was firmly planted there by every person who commented on it whenever he came into view.

Dispirited by the fact that everyone wanted a piece of her boss, and that she was no different, she was contemplating whether to have another glass of champagne or to call it a night when Logan materialised in front of her.

'I've been looking everywhere for you. Where are you going?'

Startled, Cassidy's hand fluttered to her chest. 'I was thinking of retiring for the night.'

Looking distinctly disgruntled, he shook his head. 'Not yet you're not. You've danced with every other man here tonight. Now it's my turn.'

CHAPTER NINE

CASSIDY BERATED HERSELF when she automatically put her hand in Logan's. She was so use to doing what he asked that she didn't stop to question whether it was a good idea to dance with him, and before she could reconsider he'd swept her into his arms and out onto the dance floor.

And then she couldn't really think at all with Logan's large hand planted firmly against the centre of her back and one of hers captive in his other one as he pulled her against him.

Breathlessly aware that her composure had deserted her, she tried to stop her body from melting against his but it wasn't easy when all he did was firm his hold on her when she tried to ease back.

'Relax,' he ordered, his warm breath against her ear, sending rivulets of pleasurable pulses down the line of her neck.

Cassidy lifted her gaze to find that he was staring down at her with a dangerous gleam in his eyes. 'We're just dancing.'

It didn't feel as if they were *just dancing*, and she

couldn't relax. 'I can't,' she said, wriggling a little in his grasp. 'You're holding me too close.'

'Stop trying to get away and I won't.'

Taking a breath, she did as he suggested, only to find that instead of easing his grip he inched her closer.

'I thought you said—'

'Dancing is much better when it's done in silence,' he murmured, his hand smoothing down her spine to rest on her lower back.

Her breath hitched in her chest at the caress, every one of her senses in a silent battle of wills with her self-preservation instincts. 'Your guests are already wondering why I'm here,' she said, ignoring his edict to keep quiet. 'If you don't let me have enough room to breathe, you'll start unnecessary gossip.'

And Cassidy knew intimately that gossip could destroy a person's reputation, and that Logan in particular could not afford to create any for himself. Arrantino stocks had not only started to recover once Logan had confirmed that he would become King but had bounced even higher than before.

'You have room to breathe,' he said.

Yes, she did, but every time she drew air into her lungs her breasts brushed against his jacket and it only made her want to press closer.

Realising that she would give too much away if she kept complaining, and that he was completely unaffected by how closely they were dancing, she gave up.

'Such a heavy sigh.' His lips quirked as he studied her. 'And here you looked like you were enjoying dancing earlier in the evening.'

She had been. But that was because she hadn't felt like this in the arms of any other man. Ever. 'I thought you said dancing was better without talking,' she threw back.

Logan laughed softly, the sound rumbling from his chest and into hers. 'So I did.'

If it were possible, he drew her even closer and Cassidy had no choice but to follow his lead. And then she didn't care, her body melting against his as he expertly guided her within the tight circle of his arms. He really was an exceptional dancer, his strong thighs brushing intimately against hers as he controlled their steps.

She didn't know if it was the soft music flowing over her, too much champagne, or Logan's hard body solid and strong against hers, but the intimacy of the moment took her over and dragged her into a sensual spell that made her feel dizzy.

Worried that he'd see the effect he was having on her, she ducked her face against his chest. Logan brought the hand entwined with hers in against her cheek and Cassidy had to fight the urge to place her lips against his skin.

When she felt him stiffen against her she was mortified to realise that she hadn't just *thought* it, she'd *done* it, and the tantalising male taste of his skin was exploding across her taste buds.

Jerking back, Cassidy stood mute in the circle of his arms, her eyes wide with panic.

Logan stared down at her so intently that for a moment she thought he was going to kiss her in full view of his other guests. Then he swore softly under his breath and started to lead her off the dance floor.

Stumbling to keep up, Cassidy leaned close to him. 'Where are we going?'

'Somewhere else.' His grip on her tightened as he picked up his pace.

That somewhere else turned out to be outside, down past a thick hedge of conifers to a trellised garden bed and stone steps that continued to a high brick wall. Stopping in front of a green-painted door, he flicked a hidden latch and shifted aside so that she could precede him inside.

Cassidy was immediately assailed by the soft scent of roses and jasmine that lingered in the evening air, the perfume heady and intoxicating. Breathing deeply, her eyes closed and she forgot the reason Logan had dragged her out here.

Rose bushes stood like silvery sentries around the perimeter of the small square garden, ethereally still in the moonlight.

Mesmerised, Cassidy moved from one bush to another, taking in the shape and what she could of the colour, leaning in to smell the tightly furled blossoms.

Suddenly she sensed Logan behind her, the heat from his body warming her back, even though he wasn't touching her.

'This is a Perfume Passion,' she said, recognising the flower her father had grown in their garden before their mother had walked out. 'It's a hybrid tea known for its incredible citrusy scent.'

'All I smell is you,' Logan said, his voice deep and low.

Cassidy shivered at the hunger her body picked up in his tone. She couldn't fathom that he might actually want her as much as she wanted him, and yet every feminine instinct flooded her with the knowledge that he did. It seemed incredible. Impossible. And she daren't move in case the fragile moment was ripped away from her and revealed as a figment of her imagination.

'Cassidy?'

Her name was both a question and a command on his lips, and she didn't move as he shifted closer. If she leaned back the barest inch they'd be touching, his front to her back, his hands on her body. His warm breath on her neck. Every cell in her body urged her to do it but she couldn't. She couldn't make that tiny move to show what she wanted because the fear of making a mistake overwhelmed her.

And then Logan's hands settled gently on either side of her hips, taking the decision out of her hands.

Cassidy's breath left her lungs in an excited rush. Hearing it, Logan's fingers tightened as he nuzzled her hair aside, his lips soft as he kissed the tender skin beneath her ear. 'You taste better than I imagined.'

Cassidy shivered, arching her neck to the side, a quiver racing through her as Logan's lips seared a path to the pulse point at the base of her neck. Need flooded the space between her legs and she sagged against him.

'And you feel better than I imagined.' His hands came more fully around her, splaying across her belly and coming to rest under her raging heartbeat as he took her weight back against his chest.

Cassidy's breasts ached to have him shift his palms higher, a small keening sound ripping from her throat as he kissed the base of her neck, his teeth biting gently on the tendon that joined her shoulder. Her whole body drew tight at the contact, a stab of piercing pleasure shooting from her breasts to her core as he finally moved his hands and cupped her in his palms.

Her sob of pleasure was lost as one of his hands rose to turn her chin as his mouth captured hers. Twisting in his arms, Cassidy plastered herself up against him and wound her arms around his neck, her mouth open to the delicious thrust of his tongue.

The distant sound of crystal clinking and the soft strains of the cello couldn't compete with the sound of her heartbeat in her ears as Cassidy gave herself over to the madness of Logan's kiss.

Her father's early warning to 'hold out until you know it's real' was muddled with the bizarre feeling that this *was* real, and then her sister's voice joined the mix, urging her to soak up every experience while she was here.

But neither message mattered. All that did matter was for this madness to continue. For the clamouring in her body, and the desire to touch this man, be met.

Now,

Always.

'Logan?'

His confident mouth slanted across hers, teasing her and devouring her in turn, his tongue seducing her to open and cling. Cassidy moaned and the kiss deepened until they were both panting.

Logan leaned his forehead against hers to catch his breath. 'I don't know what this is,' he murmured, his voice like velvet-covered gravel. 'And I don't care. I want you in my bed. Tell me you want to be there too.'

The raw need behind his command sent a shiver up her spine, creating a tingling sensation that spread over her skin. She did want what he wanted. She wanted to be in his bed with a desire that terrified her because she was very afraid that she wanted it too much. If it was just a matter of physical release she might not be so perturbed, but she couldn't hide from the feeling that it was more than that, at least for her.

'Cassidy?' His lips grazed her ear lobe, his warm breath sending her brain into free fall. 'Tell me.'

'Yes.' Her arms tightened around his neck as she gave herself over to a need that was greater than fear. 'Yes, I want to be in your—oh!'

Even before the words were out of her mouth he was lifting her and striding toward the entrance to the rose garden. Overawed at the powerful muscles in his shoulders that flexed beneath her hands, all Cassidy could do was bury her head against his shoulder and hang on.

Logan didn't know how he made it to his apartments without being seen by anyone other than the two guards stationed outside his door but he didn't care. He didn't care about anything right now but the woman in his arms and the ache in his body. He hadn't meant this to happen, hadn't *expected* it to happen, but now that it was he knew he needed it more than he'd ever needed anything.

'Cassidy?'

She looked up at him, her moss-green eyes soft, her body pliant in his arms. He groaned and bent to her, taking her mouth in another deep, hungry kiss.

Her fingers slid into his hair and Logan was beyond reason, completely lost to the feel and the taste of her, the soft curve of her body in his arms. The trickle of worry that perhaps he needed her just a little too much was replaced by the burning desire to strip her naked.

He released her legs so that her body slid down his, but he didn't let her touch the floor. His hands banded around her as he continued to devour her mouth, one hand sliding lower to cup her bottom, the other moving up to the back of her head, his fingers tangling in the silky mass of her auburn hair.

Cassidy writhed against him, the little sounds of pleasure coming from her lips driving his need higher.

Conceding that if he didn't leash his lust for her this would be all over in a matter of minutes, Logan dragged air into his lungs and stood her beside his bed.

She looked at him with glazed eyes and he leaned forward and took her mouth in another addictive kiss.

A little moan escaped her lips and he realised that he already loved those sounds. That he wanted more. Smoothing his hands down over her narrow shoulders, he skimmed his fingers down her arms, revelling in the way she shivered beneath his touch. She was so responsive, so expressive, and so *his*.

Suddenly impatient to see all of her, Logan searched

for the zipper in her dress and eased it down. The bodice sagged to her waist, revealing gorgeous breasts cupped in a whisper of silk.

'You wore it,' he breathed, tracing his fingers gently along the delicate edge of the cup, making her tremble.

'It came with the dress,' she said, angling to get closer to him.

Logan held her back so that he could look at her. 'I know. I chose it.'

'You did?' Her eyes flew to his. 'I thought the shop assistant would have done that.'

'Not a chance, *mi amor*. I've been imagining you in this all night and reality far exceeds what I came up with.'

Her hands rose as if to shield herself, but Logan captured them in his. Then he sat on the bed and pulled her between his spread thighs.

Cupping her breasts in his hands, he watched her eyes glaze over with pleasure as the rough pads of his thumbs grazed her nipples.

The catch in her breath sent a spike of heat through his blood and he bent forward, kissing his way towards one rigid peak before pulling it into his mouth. She moaned, a soft keening sound, her hands forking into his hair, her grip urging him on.

Logan was happy to oblige her, his lips and tongue caressing each hard bud in turn as he teased her arousal to another level.

'Logan?'

She twisted in his arms, arching closer, and he gave her what she craved, unclipping the bra at the back and letting if fall away before he fully latched onto her nipple and tugged hard.

Her fingers tensed in his hair, her head thrown back as she gasped with delight.

He was delighted himself, her response ratcheting up his own arousal until it was all he could do not to throw her onto the bed and bury himself inside her.

But he was enjoying unwrapping her too much, which he continued doing, sliding the dress down her legs so that it pooled at her feet. This time it was his breath that caught as he took in her slender legs and the pale silk at the juncture of her thighs.

A soft curse left his throat and his hands shook a little as he took her hips between his hands and eased the scanty fabric downwards.

'Logan…' Her soft plea for more undid him and he eased one hand up the inside of her creamy thigh, while the other one held her in place.

'Are you wet for me, Cassidy?' His voice was thick with need, his eyes on hers as his fingers grazed her softness.

A whimper escaped her throat and her feet shifted wider, giving him better access to her. He took it, cupping her sweet mound in his hand, the essence of her damp against his palm.

She wasn't just wet, she was fully aroused, her female scent sending his senses into a spin.

Growling softly, Logan pushed to his feet, picking her up and throwing her on the bed before she had time to draw breath.

She gave a nervous laugh and glanced at her feet. 'My heels—'

'Leave them.' He circled her ankles with his fingers and slowly parted her thighs.

'Logan, it's too much,' she said, her cheeks flushing even hotter under his gaze.

'Let me,' he said, coming over the top of her and bracing his hands on either side of her head. 'I want to taste you.'

'I don't… I've never…' her tongue sneaked out to wet her lips and Logan kissed her as he wondered just how innocent she was.

'You mean no man has ever gone down on you before?'

She shook her head, her hair spread out on his white sheets.

'Then it will be my pleasure to introduce you to the delights of the flesh, *mi amor*,' he said, chuckling a little as she tried to grip his shoulder to prevent him from sliding down her body to bury his face between her legs.

Her gasp of shock turned to one of rapture as he swept his tongue along the seam of her lips, his hands urging her thighs to spread as her hesitation dissolved.

He took a moment to breathe her in and then he showed her exactly what she'd been missing, using every ounce of expertise he had to bring her to the brink of climax over and over before finally letting her fall over the edge into delirious oblivion.

She screamed his name as she orgasmed, her fingernails making small crescent moons in his shoulders.

Logan didn't mind. His body was throbbing and he barely gave her any time to recover before his clothing hit the floor and he'd rolled a condom over his pulsing erection.

She took him in as he came over the top of her, her hands skimming his shoulders and stroking his chest.

'I want to touch you,' she said.

'Next time,' he promised, his lips taking her mouth in a searing kiss as he positioned himself at her entrance. 'I need to be inside you too badly to wait for that.'

He stroked a hand down over her thigh and around to her bottom to angle her up to him and then he entered her on one deep, smooth thrust.

He felt her body tense beneath his, a frown forming between his eyes as he gazed down at her. 'Cassidy?'

'Oh, that feels so full,' she moaned, wriggling her hips tentatively beneath him as if she was trying to get comfortable.

'You have done this before, haven't you?' he asked, straining to hold himself back.

'Yes.' Her gaze swept him in wonder. 'Once. But it was nothing like this.'

Once?

He wanted to pursue that incredible detail, but she'd started moving, shattering his concentration. 'Cassidy, *mi amor*, you need to relax. That's right, you're so tight.'

He groaned as her inner muscles gave around his hard length, her lower body tilting upwards as she sought to take him even deeper.

Sweat rolled down his spine as he powered inside her, swallowing her gasp of pleasure with his kiss. Sensation built like a dam about to burst as she learned his rhythm and matched him, her legs locking around his hips in an attempt to find her release. He wasn't at all sure he could hold out until she got there again, and then she did, her body exploding around his in a paroxysm of pleasure that shredded his self-control and sent him spiralling into the strongest climax he'd ever had.

Fighting for breath, Logan rested on top of her, completely shattered, a rush of pure emotion short-circuiting his brain.

Time had no meaning as his lungs worked to regulate his breathing, the soft rasps of her own uneven breaths warming his throat, her slim arms loose around his shoulders.

Sex had always been great for Logan, fantastic even, but this… What they'd just shared together was something entirely different. And for a man who prided himself on control and a keen ability to keep emotion and sex separate he'd just displayed an unhealthy version of the opposite. Because that had not felt controlled, or unemotional.

Waiting for his usual desire to remove himself immediately from a woman's arms, he was surprised when it didn't happen.

Then he heard Cassidy's soft sound of shock and knew that at least one of them was panicking.

Sensing that she was about to push him away, Logan rolled to his side and drew the length of her body against his. 'What's wrong? Did I hurt you?'

He hadn't been overly rough, but he hadn't exactly been gentle either.

Cassidy buried her head against his chest. 'No. But I should go.'

'Why?'

'Because…because… I'm in your bed.'

'Which is where I want you to stay,' he said, realising that it was true. 'Tell me how it is that you've only had sex once?'

She made an inarticulate sound of discomfort. 'Because the first time wasn't something I felt compelled to repeat.'

'Why?' Logan's muscles immediately tensed. 'Did he hurt you?'

'No.' Her voice was muffled against his chest. 'He was repaying me for giving him my study notes.'

Logan reared back to look at her. 'You bartered sex for study notes?'

'Not deliberately.' Even in the low light he caught the scarlet tinge to her cheeks. 'I thought he liked me.'

'Idiot.'

'Well, thanks.' She made to push away from him but he hauled her back.

'Not you. Him. He clearly had no idea what he was missing out on.'

'He did know because we—'

'He didn't. He obviously had no idea how to arouse you.' Logan rolled onto his back and brought her over the top of him. She looked down at him in surprise, her palms flat against his chest, her hair a curtain framing her lovely face. 'Widen your legs.'

'Logan—'

'Do it,' he whispered, settling her thighs on either side of his hips so that she could feel exactly how much she turned him on.

'Oh!'

'Yes.'

Reaching up Logan dragged her mouth down to his, plastering her upper body to his chest. 'Let me love you again. You're so beautiful, *mi amor.*'

'Logan…' Her token resistance was lost as she gripped his face in her hands, her body supple and pliant as he showed her just how much he wanted her.

Logan woke from an almost catatonic state after a night of unbelievable sex to find himself alone. He took in the mussed bed sheets and the stream of light that arrowed between the partially closed curtains.

The whole incredible night came back to him in a rush, starting with that incredible kiss in the rose garden to the moment he'd surged inside Cassidy's body that first time. Just thinking about it sent a shaft of arousal through his bloodstream and he strained his ears to hear if she was in the shower.

Silence greeted him and he wondered where she was. On the rare occasion that he spent the whole night with a woman it was usually to wake up with her artfully displayed on the sheets beside him and ready for round two.

He frowned. He couldn't remember how many times his body had sought Cassidy's during the night but he did remember how sleepily receptive she had been each time he'd reached for her.

Hell, he'd just spent an incredible night in bed with his EA. The realisation was like a hammer blow to the solar plexus. From the moment he'd found himself attracted to her he'd planned to keep things strictly professional between them.

So much for that.

He'd been undone as soon as she'd appeared in that amazing gown in his drawing room, all his good intentions disappearing like dust in a sandstorm.

He scrubbed a hand over his face. No matter what the cause, there was no getting around the fact that he'd just made his life exponentially more complicated than it already had been.

And he'd slept with an employee. Just as his father used to do.

Leo's words bounced around inside his head. Something about Logan not being like their father because he didn't use his position as a power play with women. And his own response. *'Regardless, the only thing Cassidy and I have between us is a close professional relationship.'*

Right. Having just spent much of the night doing the most intimate things a man and a woman could do together, he could no longer lay claim to that.

And even though he hadn't used his position as her superior to get Cassidy into bed, there was no denying that he'd set aside his principles and slept with an employee.

In fact, he'd even forgotten that she was an employee. Sometime during these last few days his view of her as just his EA had transformed into something different.

He remembered her at the museum. Her warmth with those around her. Her smile. She had not only handled herself impeccably during the event, she'd added to it. He had always forced himself to only notice her professional attributes in the office, but it was clear she was much more than that. She was an accomplished, loyal woman whose commitment to her job, and her family, ran as deeply as his own.

He'd never taken the time to really know her and now he knew her a little too well. Would they be able to get their working relationship back on track? Because that was a priority. The idea of having to find a new EA as good as her didn't thrill him. But what did thrill him was the thought of seeing her again. Which didn't help.

Forcing an image of a sexy, pliant Cassidy from his mind, he jumped out of bed and trekked into his bathroom, heading straight for the shower.

A cold one.

He needed to clear his head, and lying in bed recalling every erotic moment they had shared the night before wasn't going to achieve that outcome.

The important thing to do was to set aside everything that had happened last night and chalk it up to two people who, having just discovered that they shared an intense chemistry, had given in to temptation after a particularly gruelling few days. Because he had never intended to jeopardise her position in his life and he didn't want to lose her over one slip-up.

And hopefully she felt the same way.

Hopefully she hadn't misunderstood last night and believed that sex equalled a serious relationship. It never had for him, and usually he made that clear with a woman from the outset.

So where had that speech disappeared to the night before? The same place as logic and self-control.

Slamming his hand against the controls, he stepped from the shower, shaved and pulled on jeans and a shirt.

There was no sense in putting this off. He had to find Cassidy and deliver the news that as good as last night had been it would be best for all concerned if their relationship remained that of boss and employee and nothing else.

And surely she'd want the same thing. She was a woman who liked her i's dotted and her t's crossed as much as he did.

She was also romantic, his rational side reminded him. *Romantic and inexperienced.*

And he had been the one to shift their relationship into the personal realm when he'd danced with her. He might not have used power to persuade her into his bed but he'd known how badly she'd affected him and like a moth drawn to a flame, he'd let his libido take control.

Deciding that what was required here was calm, logical reasoning, he shut down his guilt and went in search of her.

CHAPTER TEN

CASSIDY REREAD THE letter she'd just finished typing. It wasn't very long. In fact, it was quite short. Should she add more?

Your Majesty,
It has been a pleasure working for you these past twenty-one months, but I hereby tender my resignation forthwith.

Was it too blunt?

And what about the pleasure reference?

After last night she didn't want that to be misconstrued and so she deleted *'a pleasure'* for the more ambiguous *'great'*.

Then she added a couple of lines about how much she had learned, working with him, and sent it to the printer.

And even if she hadn't already been thinking of resigning there was absolutely no way she would be able to work with him after last night. Just the thought of facing him this morning was enough to make her blush.

And sleeping with her boss was not exactly what her sister had been thinking about when she'd advised her to fully immerse herself in the experience so that she had no regrets. It hadn't been what she'd been thinking either when she'd decided to attend the ball at the last minute, although she was honest enough to admit that she had wanted him to notice her as more than just his EA last night. And she *had* wanted to create some 'amazing memories'.

Mission accomplished, she thought.

Not that she regretted anything that had happened between them. How could she when it had felt so right to be in his arms? But she had to eradicate that feeling. Along with her plan to work for him for another month. Yes, she'd feel badly, not helping him settle into his new role, but after last night… She felt her throat thicken with emotion. That terrible suspicion she'd had about falling in love with him had tripled since this morning.

Just remembering how she had woken up with her body wrapped around his like Christmas paper, a smile on her face and a sense of wonder in her heart, was enough to make her break out in hives.

Last night hadn't been about love or commitment, it had been about lust and letting off steam, and she wouldn't make the mistake of thinking otherwise. And no doubt Logan wouldn't want her working for him after last night either. In fact, he'd probably be relieved to receive her resignation because it would all be neat and tidy. The way they both liked things.

'Working already.' His voice behind her sounded cool, remote. 'I'm not that hard a taskmaster, am I?'

Snapping the lid closed on her laptop, Cassidy gave a guilty start.

'It's not really work, it's—' She groaned softly when the printer started up on the bench space, drawing his attention. Before she could react Logan had crossed the room in three long strides and retrieved her letter. Scanning the page, he lifted his blue eyes to hers, his gaze glittering with an unnamed emotion that made her shiver.

'I have to say this appears to be an extreme case of morning-after regret,' he said, his voice lethally soft.

She smiled as if nothing was out of the ordinary when all she could think about was how his mouth had felt, exploring her body. 'It's not regret.' It was a simple case of self-preservation. 'I know my resignation might be a surprise, and this was certainly not the way I planned to tell you, but… I think it's for the best.'

'Do you?' He came to a stop in front of her and dropped the letter on the table. 'Exactly how did you plan to tell me?'

Shifting on her seat, she felt a pleasurable sensation pulse through her lower body, a reminder of everything they had done the night before. 'I hadn't got that far. I was still working it out. But I had already decided to resign before the ball.'

'Why?'

'Because you'll be living in Arrantino permanently and my life is in New York.'

'You could easily relocate. It's not like you have anything tying you to New York other than your sister.'

'Gee, thanks for pointing that out.'

'You know what I meant.' He ran a hand through his hair, reminding her of how thick and soft it had felt under her fingers. 'If you're worried about not seeing your family I'll happily provide you with regular trips home to visit them.'

'That's very kind of you but—'

'But this has nothing to do with logistics, does it?'

Frustrated that he wouldn't just accept her resignation at face value, Cassidy let out a controlled breath. 'I've seen you naked. You've seen me naked.' Probably not the best thing to say, given the way his eyes darkened. 'You have to admit that last night makes it impossible for us to work together.'

There was also the small situation of him having to marry and her having to be nice to a woman who would be sleeping with him every night. Something she would find too confronting for words.

'I don't admit anything of the sort. Sex, no matter how good, doesn't have to ruin our professional relationship. We're both mature adults who gave in to a moment of temptation. As long as we keep emotion out of the equation, things can go back to the way they were.'

The smile he gave her was gentle, almost tender, as if she were a small child needing to be placated.

Cassidy didn't know what made her feel worse. The fact that he could so easily dismiss what had happened between them, or the fact that she couldn't. Last night she hadn't cared that she worked for him, or that there was no chance of a future for them together, or that he would never want more from her than sex. She hadn't considered that she might already like him a little too much, or what would happen afterwards. All she'd thought about was the way he had made her feel. Beautiful. Wanted. *Sensual.*

Now she felt bereft. And she knew herself well enough to know that she would one day want more from him. So much more, and she would not let herself fall for another man who wouldn't want her back.

Determined that this time she would hold her line with Logan, she pushed her glasses closer to her face and huffed out a breath. 'I'm happy to keep emotion out of the equation,' she said, resolutely ignoring the pang in her chest that said that last night had been unforgettable. 'But I'm still resigning.'

Logan's scowl deepened, his whole demeanour one of outrage. He paced away from her, his broad shoulders rigid. 'You're being stubborn.'

Cassidy's eyebrow rose as if to say *pot...kettle* and his scowl deepened.

'We make a great team. I've never had an assistant I've worked so well with before.'

Cassidy didn't disagree with him, but knowing that her professional prowess was her most important attribute to him hurt, even though it shouldn't.

'We just need to compartmentalise what happened last night,' Logan decreed. 'Something you assured me you were extremely good at during your job interview.'

'I thought I was good at it too.' It was now very clear to her that she could strike that off her superpowers list. Or perhaps it was more that her ability, along with her intelligence, seemed to diminish to zero whenever he touched her.

'Then do it now. Better yet, come to lunch with me.'

'Lunch?' She blinked, struggling to get her head around his sudden change in topic.

'I promised Leo I would meet Elly today.'

She narrowed her eyes. 'I don't know that I should be there. I don't think it's—'

'Appropriate?' His mouth turned into a grim line. 'Probably not. But it will allow me to prove to you that we can resume a normal relationship. At the moment you're using emotion to dictate your decision and that's always a mistake.'

Cassidy frowned. 'On the contrary, I'm using logic and the knowledge that when men and women become intimate it complicates things.'

'That doesn't have to be the case if both parties are mature adults.'

'Then why have you never slept with one of your EAs before? Because I'm pretty sure there were some offers on the table.'

Logan's nostrils flared, his gaze drifting to the sofa behind her. She had the distinct feeling that he was contemplating lifting her onto it and having his way with her again. The fact that she wanted that to happen so badly only convinced her that she had made the right call. She couldn't work with him. If there was one thing Cassidy knew from a childhood full of instability it was when to cut and run. Her mother had been the first person to reject her and she had been watching people walk away from her ever since. Something most of them did with startling ease. Something Logan would eventually do as well.

'If you must know, I've never been tempted before.'

Rather than feel flattered by his soft words, a lump formed in her throat because it didn't matter how tempted he had been the night before, he still only wanted her in his life as an employee. And he would never want more than that from her because not only did she not have the right pedigree to suit his new station in life, she didn't have a pedigree at all.

She swallowed heavily, ignoring the fact that even scowling and dominant he made her feel dizzy with lust. 'I won't change my mind about this,' she declared with stubborn emphasis. 'I'm not as practised as you are in being able to move on from sex. And besides that, I want to work for someone who is less demanding than you are.'

Logan made a scoffing sound. 'You'd be bored within an hour.'

Probably, but she wouldn't give him the satisfaction of agreeing with him. It would only fortify his position. 'Believe what you want.'

'Dammit, Cassidy…' He stalked to the windows that overlooked rich, rolling green hills. 'Whether you admit it or not, your resignation is rash. This is all just a matter of self-control and discipline. We make a great team. Come with me to lunch and, if at the end of the day, you're not convinced that we can work together then I'll not only accept your resignation, I'll have Ben fly you back to New York tonight.'

Cassidy gnawed on the inside of her lip. Perhaps

she should go with him if for no other reason than to prove him wrong. And, really, what was the harm? She knew she wouldn't change her mind about working for him in the future.

'This isn't a good idea,' she declared, questioning her sanity as he moved back to stop in front of her.

'Duly noted.' He adjusted her glasses on her nose as if he couldn't help himself. 'Dress is casual.'

Cassidy stared dubiously at the small red moped in the underground garage. 'We're taking that?'

Logan gave her a sexy grin. 'Not enough speed for you, *mi amor*?'

'It's not that.' She wondered what it was he was calling her and then decided that she didn't want to know. 'I'm just surprised that you would choose to ride one.'

'That's the whole point.' He swung his leg over the small contraption and balanced it between his long legs, managing to retain every ounce of his masculinity in the process. 'Sometimes, when we were younger, Leo and I would take off for a break from palace life and no one was any the wiser.'

'And security was okay with that?' She took the shiny silver helmet he proffered. 'They're okay with it now?'

'No, but they work for me. Which means they have no choice.' He grinned at her when she shook her head. 'They also know that I'm only going half an hour out of the city and I've already cleared where we're going. If something goes wrong they can be there in five minutes by helicopter. But who is going to be looking for the new King of Arrantino today, especially on one of these? Most people will assume I'm still in bed.'

At the mention of bed Cassidy's cheeks heated and she stuck her helmet on her head, accepting that he was probably right. She was accepting a lot from him lately. First the gown, then the casual outfit she had pulled from one of the designer bags in her room. And even though she intended to pay him back every cent for anything that she wore, she still cautioned herself to be careful. This wasn't a courtship by any stretch of the imagination. He wasn't in love with her, he was merely working to get the outcome he desired—which was for her to remain as his EA.

Forcing herself to not focus on the negatives and to just enjoy herself, she slung her leg over the back of the bike. Logan kicked up the stand and they zoomed out of the garage towards the rear entrance reserved for deliveries and staff.

Five minutes later they were weaving in and out of traffic and heading for the hills.

Finally dragging her eyes away from his broad back, she scanned the lush countryside rich with vineyards and orange groves.

In what felt like way too little time they pulled up outside a small house nestled behind a brick fence.

'Your brother has been staying here?'

'No. Elly lives here.' He took their helmets and slung them over the handlebars. 'Leo has been staying in a rented apartment close by. Since no one has been able to identify the woman in the photographs, her privacy has been preserved.'

'Something I'm sure she's more than happy about.'

'We will see.'

She heard the hard edge that entered his tone and placed her hand on his arm. 'You said that Elly is an archaeologist. Is there anything else I should know?'

'She's a single mother.'

'Oh, that's hard. Do you know what happened to her husband?'

'No idea. She probably dumped him for a bigger fish.'

Cassidy frowned. 'That's terribly cynical. What makes you say that? Is it because of your father?'

'No. It's because of Leo's first wife. Anastasia was a shark with red lipstick. She wanted the power and privilege that comes with being a queen but not the everyday acts of service the role requires. When she got bored she searched for entertainment elsewhere.'

'Ah.' Cassidy remembered the stylish blonde from the time she had visited Logan's New York office. A shark with red lipstick was a fitting description; the woman's blue eyes had never been still, always sizing things up. Especially Logan. At the time Cassidy had thought that her reaction had been that of any other woman in Logan's presence, but apparently all those sexy little smiles had been a tad more targeted than that. Which was even more appalling considering she had been married to his brother at the time. 'That would have made it uncomfortable for you whenever you and Leo got together.'

'Extremely. I tried to warn him about her but he

wouldn't listen and over time she succeeded in driving a wedge between us. I don't want that to happen again.'

'It doesn't mean that it will, though.'

'No. But it doesn't mean that it won't either.'

Completely understanding why Logan was preparing himself for the worst, and why he would want to protect his brother so much after having watched him battle leukaemia, Cassidy followed him as he pushed open the squeaky metal gate.

As soon as she stepped into the garden and spied the sunflower-yellow front door, Cassidy knew that Elly wouldn't be the kind of person Logan imagined her to be.

No polished sophisticate who had money as their number one goal would have such a happy front door, or a garden grown wild with lavender and poppies, neither would she have the well-worn gardening shoes placed haphazardly beside the front door that signified that she wasn't afraid to get her hands dirty.

'I know you're anticipating the worst, but Leo comes across as a smart guy,' she offered, hoping to reassure him as she stopped beside him on the veranda. 'I'm sure he knows what he's doing.'

'Marrying Anastasia goes against that theory. And they say that love is blind. Today I plan to make sure he hasn't made a second mistake before this relationship goes any further.'

Cassidy swallowed at the laser-like intensity behind Logan's blue eyes, seriously glad that she wasn't the one in the firing line. 'And if you decide she's not good for him?'

'This time I'll make sure he listens.'

'Just…' Cassidy waved her hands between them wondering if he would welcome her counsel.

'What?' he bit out with barely concealed impatience. 'You've never been backward in giving me your opinion before.'

Actually, she had, but that had usually been to do with the women he'd dated and she'd determinedly told herself it was none of her business.

'Just watch the, you know, juggernaut face, it's very intimidating.'

Both exasperated and fascinated by his EA, who apparently was determined that she was not going to be his EA for much longer, Logan found himself tense up as he waited for the door to be opened.

He wanted this to work out for his brother and he hoped Leo was right about Elly because Anastasia had made him miserable, and as far as Logan was concerned, Leo had suffered enough in his life. On top of that, these past few days had shown him how much he had missed his brother's friendship and he didn't want to lose it again so soon.

Being back home, he had come to appreciate how unfulfilled his life in New York had been, driven by making deals and moving from one success to another without really taking the time to celebrate any of it.

He glanced at Cassidy as she bent to stroke the fur of a giant ginger cat. The large feline wove between her ankles, rubbing its scent on her and purring with delight at the attention.

He knew how it felt. Right now he wanted to ditch lunch, bundle Cassidy up, stick her on the back of the moped and haul her off to the closest bedroom.

Usually after he'd spent the night with a woman he was unaffected by whether he saw her again or not, but the thought of not seeing Cassidy, of not touching her, made his gut tighten with an emotion that felt peculiarly like dread.

But he was going to have to push that aside if he was serious about fulfilling his promise and proving that with a little self-control and discipline they could easily get their relationship back on track.

Looking at her now, her gorgeous curves encased in denim and a purple gypsy blouse that he was almost certain was concealing a black bra, he wasn't at all confident that he could—or that he even wanted to.

'Hello! Welcome!'

A petite dark-haired woman and the mouth-watering aroma of homemade bread and tomato sauce greeted them. Elly's brown eyes were open and friendly and she was dressed as casually as he and Cassidy were. Score one for Elly, he thought, and then caught the cynical thought before it could progress any further. *Possibly* he was still a little jaded from his past, and *possibly* he did need to let that go and move on at some point.

'It's so nice to meet you both.'

Cassidy greeted the other woman with a natural exuberance he just didn't have, kissing her warmly on both cheeks. This in turn seemed to relax Elly and Logan masked his scowl and tried to play nice.

Fortunately Leo came up behind the woman and placed a hand on her shoulder.

'Right on time,' he said, easing the rising tension between them all with grace and aplomb.

It was a trait he was going to have to cultivate in his new role, Logan thought grimly.

And then a small ray of sunshine stepped out from behind Leo's legs with large unwavering eyes in a small fey face surrounded by clouds of dark hair.

'I'm Skylar,' she said, sticking out her hand for him to shake. 'I'm six years old. Are you Leo's brother?'

'Yes.' He found his throat had closed over and had to clear it before he could go on. Leo had sent him a text explaining that Skylar had no idea that they were from the royal family and would he mind playing along with that. Having wondered if that had been a ploy of his new girlfriend's, Logan felt a wave of shame flood him.

If the colourful array of flowers in the well-loved garden hadn't served to convince him that he was using a crooked lens with which to view the world, then this intelligent eyed child had finished the job.

Feeling unmoored for the first time in his life, he was at a loss as to how to proceed when Cassidy tucked her hand into his.

'Yes, his name is Logan, and I'm Cassidy,' she answered. 'What grade are you in at school?'

'One.'

'And what's your favourite subject?'

'Reading.'

'Ah, mine too.' Cassidy laughed. 'Ever read *Fantastic Mr Fox*?'

'Yes, twice.' Skylar beamed under Cassidy's warm interest.

'That's one of my favourites too,' Logan said, vaguely remembering that he had enjoyed the antics of the wily fox raiding Farmer Boggis's hen house. 'What?' He gave Cassidy a superior look when her eyes went wide. 'You're not the only bookworm in the house.'

Skylar giggled and ran off, muttering about books, and Elly warned them that they had started something they might regret.

Leo stepped back for them to enter the house and Logan followed everyone into the cosy cottage awash with multicoloured cushions on the sofa and quirky prints on the walls.

Elly moved to the table set with a candelabrum and ceramic bowls filled with olives and dip and picked up a bottle of wine just as a timer went off in the kitchen.

Slightly flustered, she glanced around and Leo gave her a nod. 'I'll do the wine…you check the chicken.'

Elly's face immediately softened and she let out a slow breath of relief.

Leo touched her face so briefly that if Logan had blinked he would have missed it, but he hadn't and he felt a tug inside his chest at having witnessed the tender moment.

Cassidy shifted beside him, a dreamy smile on her

face, and he realised with a pang that this was what she most likely wanted from a man.

Love.

Probably a family too.

The whole concept was so foreign to him that he was relieved when Skylar danced back into the room with an armload of books and readily sat down to view her offerings.

Slightly embarrassed that he was using a child to mask the raw emotions that seemed keen on piercing his skin, he soon got caught up in the relaxed atmosphere and started to enjoy the afternoon.

'Thanks.'

Logan glanced away from where Skylar was teaching Cassidy some sort of game on the outdoor patio. He was quite sure his EA knew how to play it already, but was indulging the high-spirited child.

'What are you thanking me for?' he asked, taking in his brother's relaxed demeanour.

'Meeting Elly and Skylar on their level and not bringing your prejudices to the door.'

Logan shifted uncomfortably, well aware that if Cassidy hadn't spoken to him about his 'juggernaut' face before Elly had opened the door, the outcome of the day might have been very different. 'I did bring my prejudices to the door,' he admitted with a wry grimace. 'Cassidy made me leave them there.'

Leo laughed. 'I knew I liked that woman. I'll be sure to thank her in our wedding speech.'

Logan shook his head. 'You're that serious about Elly?'

'I gave up the crown for her, didn't I?'

Logan sighed heavily. 'You did. And I'm man enough to acknowledge when I'm wrong.'

'So no warning?' Leo asked bemusedly.

'No warning,' Logan grouched. 'She seems great. And it's good to see you happy.'

'And you.'

Logan frowned. 'What do you mean?'

Leo shrugged. 'It's been a long time since I've seen you without your phone glued to your ear or pushing another deal through. It's a nice change.'

Before Logan could fully process his brother's observations Skylar's clear voice called out to them. 'Who wants to play hopscotch?'

Hopscotch?

Leo laughed at his flummoxed expression and Logan elbowed his brother in the ribs.

'I'd love to,' he said. 'And so would Leo.'

Leo elbowed him back and placed his glass of wine on the table. 'Prepare to have your arse whipped,' he promised.

An hour later, with Skylar victorious, Logan downed a glass of cold water as Cassidy came up beside him at the kitchen bench. The sun had started to lower in the sky, taking some of the heat out of the air.

'Skylar's really tired. It might be a good time to head back,' she murmured.

Logan nodded in agreement, dragging her delicate

scent into his lungs and wanting nothing more than to tug on her ponytail to bring her mouth to his. He hadn't touched her all day but now he wanted to. Badly. And he didn't care if that broke his promise or not. Having her as his EA was suddenly far less important than having her in his arms.

After saying their goodbyes Cassidy settled on the moped behind him and put her hands around his waist, and Logan knew he wasn't ready to return to the palace, or his new life, just yet.

CHAPTER ELEVEN

'Where are we?'

Cassidy glanced around at the small car park high up in the hills overlooking the Mediterranean. The late afternoon sunlight turned the blond streaks in Logan's hair to gold before he covered the thick layers with a baseball cap he'd grabbed from under the seat of the moped.

'It's called Gran Mundo Lookout. It's one of the most beautiful places in Arrantino. Let me show you why.'

Conscious that they were not the only people on the gravel trail, Cassidy ducked her head and clung to Logan's hand as he led her along the path.

'Relax,' he advised. 'You're very expressive and you look like you you've just robbed a bank, which will make anyone watching us nervous.'

'But what if you're recognised?' she hissed under her breath.

'Most of the people here are tourists who wouldn't have a clue who I am. I'm not worried. So you shouldn't be either.'

Unconvinced, because it was her nature to worry, Cassidy tried her best to look unconcerned. Logan might be right about the tourists not recognising him, but he clearly didn't understand how appealing he was *as a man*, and she'd already noticed a couple of women giving him covetous glances as they crunched along the path.

'*Gran mundo* means great world,' he explained as they rounded a corner and Cassidy let out a reverent breath as the leafy foliage they'd passed through opened up to reveal an endless rugged coastline dotted here and there with colourful fishing villages nestled along the coast like jewels hanging from a golden chain.

'Wow,' she murmured softly, taking in the terraced vineyards and the ancient buildings that looked like they might topple from the rocky cliff face and straight into the azure sea at any moment. 'It's gorgeous.' She turned her face to his with delight. 'Thank you for bringing me here.'

'It's my pleasure.' His voice had a rough edge that instantly sent spirals of need cascading inside her.

All day he had been a perfect gentleman, not touching her, as he had promised, and it had driven her insane. Especially when he had allowed himself to be coaxed into a game of hopscotch by a playful six-year-old. Before long they had all been playing the game, Leo and Logan naturally turning it into a testosterone-fuelled competition of who could best the other.

'What are you grinning about?'

He stepped closer to her, a certain glint in his eye heating her blood even more.

'I was remembering the game of hopscotch after lunch. It was nice of you to indulge Skylar. Especially since you had already read her favourite book to her before lunch.'

Logan shrugged. 'I like her. The kid is so precocious I might offer her a position on my special council one day. To say that Leo will definitely have his hands full with that one is a gross understatement.'

'So you think that he and Elly might work out?'

He saw the impish grin that crossed her face and tugged on the end of her ponytail. 'Do you want to hear me say I was wrong?'

'Yes.' Her eyes sparkled. 'It would be such a novelty. But truly I completely get why you were worried. I feel the same way about Peta. That day everything went wrong in your office I was reeling from the shock that she was engaged. I never imagined that she could trust someone enough to marry him after everything she's been through. It seems like such a leap of faith, but the fact is she's more of an optimist than I am. She thinks love is worth the gamble.'

Something in her eyes, a shadow of sorts, poked at the hard, solid barrier around his heart. 'Maybe she's right.'

'You're agreeing?' She gave a startled laugh, shaking her head. 'Now I've definitely heard it all.'

Logan moved closer so that he was blocking everything from her view but him. 'Want to hear something else I might have been wrong about?'

'What?'

Her voice was breathless with anticipation. 'That we'd be able to resume our normal working relationship after last night.'

'You don't think we can?'

'No.' He took another step closer, effectively caging her in against the wooden safety barrier. 'Do you?'

'No.' Her throat bobbed as she swallowed. 'But I already knew that because… I… No, I don't think we can.'

Logan tilted her chin up so that her eyes met his. 'You were going to say something else. What was it?'

'Nothing.' She shook her head emphatically. 'But I know I can't work for you and I don't want you to try and change my mind because I always cave in to what you want.'

'I don't intend to try and change your mind.' He slipped his hand around to cradle the nape of her neck. 'And now that we've established that you no longer work for me, I don't have to worry about breaking any more rules with you.'

He nuzzled a few loose strands of her hair away from her neck, bracing his legs wide as he leaned in to kiss her.

She immediately opened to him, her small hands warm as she flattened them against his chest.

A low moan escaped from deep inside his chest as she responded to him, her hands moving up over his shoulders, her fingers tangling in the hair at the base of his cap. Feeling her unrestrained response, Logan put his arms around her waist and gathered her up against him.

The kiss went from 'exploratory' to 'get a room' within seconds and it was only a deeply ingrained sense of decorum from years of looking over his shoulder that had him pulling back.

Without her glasses Cassidy's green eyes were like luminous pools of phosphorescence. Unable to hold back, he dipped his head and kissed her again. This time when he came up for air she leaned her forehead against his chest, panting softly.

'I thought you said this was just a matter of self-control and discipline,' she said breathlessly.

'It is,' he said against her ear, absorbing her delicate shudder deep inside his body. 'But I'm all out. You?'

When she glanced up at him he read the answering response in her diluted pupils and this time he didn't need her verbal okay. It was written all over her gorgeous face. 'I'm not sure I ever had any.'

Cassidy glanced around at the front of the secluded sandstone building Logan had pulled up in front of. She was already having doubts about the intelligence of agreeing to sleep with him again but it was so easy to stem the trickle of unease.

He made her feel sexy and irresistible and she was simply intoxicated by the thought of exploring the chemistry between them once more. Reality would intrude at some point and she'd deal with it then but for now...

She glanced over as Logan secured the bike beside

the brick wall. 'I thought we were going back to the palace?'

He pulled his helmet from his head and stowed it with hers on the bike. 'You know when I said that a king rarely has any privacy? At times it will feel so oppressive it will be claustrophobic. But right now I have a moment. A weekend. And I don't want to spend it at the palace where I'll be available to anyone who wants me. Tonight I'm going to turn off my phone and do what I want to do.'

'You make it sound like it will be the last time that can ever happen.'

'It won't be the last—it is possible to sneak away now and then, and even the King gets holidays—but the weight of responsibility will never be far away, and I'll always be on call.'

'So what is this place?' She looked up at high arched windows that denoted the buildings of Moorish heritage.

'My cousin's apartment. He's in Tahiti, surfing, right now so he won't mind if we use it.'

'He might not but I can't see your security detail letting you stay here without first making sure it's secure.'

'I know.'

Just then the ancient wooden door to the interior garden opened towards them and two soldiers with machine guns strapped across their torsos stepped outside.

'All clear, Your Majesty,' the female soldier said, taking the lead.

'Thank you. I'll let you know tomorrow when we're ready to return.'

Moving with a lightness that belied the weight of their heavy-duty equipment, the soldiers left them alone.

Curious to see what a surfer's place would look like, Cassidy followed Logan along a stone path dotted with green ferns into an elevator that took them to the top floor. The apartment didn't disappoint. Low sofas in burnt orange, dark square tiles on the floor, a magnificent view of the white yachts in the harbour from the arched windows. When she looked closer she could see that all the appliances were state of the art, and ready on command, as evidenced when jazz music filtered into the room through hidden speakers at Logan's voiced request.

'Do the curtains also open and close on command?' she asked, moving into the kitchen and perching on the edge of a wicker stool.

'Of course.' Logan popped the cork on a bottle of wine he'd pulled from the wine fridge. 'My cousin loves his gadgets.'

He poured them two glasses and raised a toast. 'To secret rendezvous.'

Cassidy's heart did a mini-somersault inside her chest, her gaze dropping to his mouth.

The air between them became charged and Logan slowly lowered his glass to the bench top. Then he rounded the counter and took hers from fingers that had turned nerveless.

Without preamble or finesse he lifted her onto the counter and reached up to drag her mouth down to his.

Cassidy felt like her body went up in flames, her

fingernails digging into his thick, soft hair, her moans trapped in her throat as he fed her kiss after kiss.

'Por Dios, Cassidy... Mi hermosa mujer... Mi amor...'

Logan's litany of Arrantinian love words tightened her nipples into unbearably aching peaks.

Feeling wanton and unlike herself—or maybe more like herself than ever before—she raised her arms and dragged her blouse up over her head, letting it flutter to the counter behind her.

Logan's eyes were hooded as he watched her, his gaze hot as it travelled from her face to her collarbone, his fingers trailing gently after, raising goose bumps wherever he touched her.

'Take your hair down,' he encouraged, his tone low and deep.

Cassidy did, letting the soft waves fall down around her shoulders, relishing the way he hissed out a low breath before hands forked into the mass as he pulled her lips back to his.

Hot liquid need pooled between Cassidy's thighs and she shifted restlessly on the counter, needing more.

Reading her perfectly, Logan pulled his mouth from hers and buried it against her neck, licking and sucking at her skin.

Burning up with need, she suddenly felt self-conscious sitting in the bright sunlight in only her jeans and a black bra. But then he looked at her with such undisguised hunger it made all her inhibitions dissolve to dust. 'You have too many clothes on,' she murmured, tugging at his T-shirt.

Obliging her, he reefed it over his head with one

hand and she immediately smoothed her hand over the pelt of thick hair on his chest.

He groaned huskily, bending to her once more and trailing hot kisses down between her breasts.

Breathless, she cried out in pleasure as his lips crested one breast and sucked her nipple deeply into his mouth.

'Logan.' She gripped his wide shoulders, dazed with rapture as he removed her bra and feasted directly on her naked flesh, his lips pulling first one peak into his mouth with wicked skill before moving to the other and then back again.

Delirious with wanting, all she could do was hold on, barely aware when he picked her up and carried her to the sofa. He placed her on it and stood in front of her, unbuckling his belt, his blue eyes so hot they threatened to incinerate her.

Feeling more daring than she ever had before, Cassidy leaned forward and brushed his fingers aside. 'Let me.'

He went still, every one of his senses homed in on her trembling fingers as she released his zipper and pushed his jeans and briefs down his legs. He was gorgeous. So perfect she felt her heart constrict. Reaching out, she enclosed the long, hard length of him in her hand, her eyes finding his to gauge if he was enjoying her touch.

His chest moved in and out like a set of bellows, his eyes half-lidded as he gazed down at her.

Turning her attention back to his thick erection, she leaned forward and greedily flicked him with her tongue, fascinated by the low growl that emanated from deep inside his chest.

'Cassidy…' His fingers tangled in her hair and she looked up at him. 'Stop torturing me, *mi amor.*'

So turned on it was shocking, Cassidy slid his long length between her lips, completely lost to everything but pleasuring him.

What felt like seconds later, Logan released her hair and shuffled her back. About to complain, Cassidy fell silent at the feral glitter she saw in his eyes.

He reached down and nearly tore her jeans in half as he yanked them from her body. Then he was on her, his fingers sliding between their bodies, parting her swollen folds before he drove them deep inside her body.

Cassidy nearly blacked out at the pleasure, only dimly aware that he had sheathed himself before he'd moved between her thighs and opened her to the hot, hard plunge of his body. Each powerful thrust moved her closer and closer to the peak of pleasure until the only thing she could say was his name over and over as her body splintered into a thousand pieces.

Minutes felt like they turned into days as she lay there, gasping for breath. Logan reached around her back and gathered her up against him. Cassidy looped her arms around his neck, her limbs the consistency of overcooked spaghetti.

'Damn.' He pressed his forehead to hers. 'I didn't mean that to happen.'

Cassidy blinked up at him. 'You didn't?'

'No.' His brow puckered. 'I meant to at least make it to the bedroom.' He feathered light kisses across her eyelids. 'But you affect me so badly I have no control where you're concerned. How hungry are you?'

'You mean for food?' She was so full after the enormous lunch they had not long eaten that she didn't care if she didn't eat for a week.

A slow grin crossed Logan's face. He stood up and reached for her hand, pulling her to her feet and giving her a quick, blistering kiss. 'Neither am I.'

'Tell me about growing up in Ohio.'

Logan pushed the midnight feast of olives and cheese, which they had assembled after raiding his cousin's larder, onto the floor and stretched out on the bed beside her.

She rolled her eyes at his unabashed nudity and fixed the sheet tighter beneath her arms. He hid a grin, knowing that all he would have to do to make her soft and begging was to drag that sheet down and take one of her lovely breasts into his mouth.

Deciding that he could forgo the pleasure of her body for at least another ten minutes, he played with a strand of her hair instead.

She glanced up at him, her long lashes causing soft shadows to fall over her cheekbones. 'What do you want to know?'

'Anything—' *and everything* '—you want to tell me.'

She started talking about the weatherboard house she had grown up in on the outskirts of a small town called Sherwent Creek, her mother walking out on them when she was fifteen and what that had meant to them all. 'My sister and my father really suffered after she left. It wasn't long after that my sister fell pregnant, then my father, who had already been struggling, completely fell apart…' Her voice grew quiet. 'Being the oldest, I did my best to cook and clean and make sure Peta was okay, but she wasn't interested in me being a replacement parent and for a while we fell out. Then she had the twins and that was when things really got tough.' She winced and peered at him sheepishly. 'Sorry, you were probably wanted to hear about the tourist attractions rather than my life story.'

Logan brushed her lips with his. 'If I want to know about the tourist attractions I'll visit there myself. It's you who interests me. What happened next?'

'Well… Peta is quite shy and the gossip and derogatory comments she received, having the twins so young, made all of our lives miserable. Peta drifted for a while, barely making ends meet. I got a job to help out with the bills but…' She hesitated and Logan sensed she was holding something back but didn't want to push her. She blinked as if to clear her memory.

'It got so bad that our father eventually relocated us to another town. We packed up the station wagon one night and drove all through the night. Amber and April were only young at the time.' She gave a soft laugh at the memory. 'Anyway, it was a little better after that but not great. Eventually Peta moved out and I stayed to take care of our dad.'

'What happened to him?'

'He died in a car accident.'

'I'm sorry, *mi amor*. And your mother? Did she ever return?'

'No. Having kids didn't suit her. I have no idea where she is now.'

Logan felt the pain of every word she spoke like a lash abrading his skin. He wanted to grab every one of those people who had made Cassidy's life a misery around the neck and squeeze. Hard.

Unable to do that, he pulled her unyielding body against his and looped his arm around her waist. 'Then what?'

She laughed softly. 'You really want to know everything, don't you?'

'I'm greedy like that.'

Loving the way he was able to make her smile after such a gruelling story, he encouraged her to go on. 'So what's next? Was that when you moved to New York? Came to work for me?'

'Yes.' A fleeting smile crossed her face. 'Once my father passed away I moved to New York to finish my online course and Peta moved in with me. After that I needed a well-paid job and walking into your building was definitely a case of being in the right place at the right time. I never expected to get the job but just as I handed my résumé to your receptionist she became violently ill. You had a Chinese delegation waiting to receive their building passes, as well as a persistent paparazzi guy lurking around, asking questions about you. It was Todd Greene, I think.'

Logan's lips twisted into a grim line. 'Don't talk to me about him. The guy has a vendetta. He tried to get a press pass to the coronation yesterday too but I had him removed. Anyway, go on.'

Cassidy shrugged. 'There's not much else to tell. I happened to know how to use the computer system you used so I printed the passes for the Chinese delegates and phoned your HR department. Your HR manager was in a flap because you'd just fired your last assistant and demanded a replacement asap. She interviewed me on the day, did a security check, and I was hired two days later.'

'Much to everyone's relief. You know you're amazing, right?' He kissed her shoulder. 'And utterly beautiful.'

'Don't say that. I don't need those kinds of compliments to feel secure.'

At her nonchalant comment Logan's eyebrow went skyward.

'I don't,' she persisted.

'That's because you don't believe it,' he said shrewdly. 'But you are beautiful, Cassidy.'

'I'm not.' Her eyes wouldn't quite meet his. 'My sister is the beautiful one. You haven't met her but—'

'I'm sure your sister is quite lovely, but we're not talking about her. We're talking about you.' He tilted her chin up so that she was forced to look into his eyes. 'And you are gorgeous. Gorgeous eyes. Gorgeous nose.' He kissed each attribute he labelled. 'Gorgeous chin. Gorgeous neck.' His voice became a sexy murmur. 'Gorgeous collarbone. Gorgeous—'

Cassidy squealed as he slid lower down her body. 'I get the picture!'

Rising up to loom over her, his biceps braced to take his weight, he locked his gaze with hers. She touched his face, her fingers stroking over his stubble, her eyes soft. For a moment he heard nothing but the sound of his own heart beating and the echoes of forever in his head.

'When you look at me like that,' she whispered breathlessly, 'I feel like anything is possible.'

CHAPTER TWELVE

THIS TIME WHEN Logan woke up, Cassidy was beside him, her arm flung across his abdomen, her leg draped over his thigh, and for someone who was always eager to move on from a woman he'd slept with he was hard pressed to explain this sense of belonging he felt at having her nestled beside him.

He knew it was very early because no light appeared around the blinds on his windows, or it was very late. He couldn't tell. He'd lost all sense of time after he'd made love to her again, more slowly this time, wanting to eradicate all the hurts she'd experienced as a child.

He moved a strand of her hair away from her face and thought about all the reasons why it was a bad idea to continue seeing her and couldn't come up with any, not now that she no longer worked for him. Since they were both single, there was no reason they couldn't continue an affair for as long as it lasted.

Other than the fact that Cassidy seemed more determined to get away from him than to stay with him but maybe that was only because she didn't know how he felt about her.

Which raised the question—how did he feel?

He liked her. He was insanely attracted to her. But it felt like more than that. She was the smartest, sweetest, most caring woman he'd ever met. He loved it that she matched him in so many ways. In the boardroom, the bedroom and even on the gym mat. If he ever lost his fitness edge, he knew she'd cut him off at the knees, and the knowledge that he could bend her but not break her was extremely appealing.

He also wanted to protect her and take care of her. And that was definitely new. He'd always avoided engaging his emotions with women in the past. Sex had always been just sex, but he was struggling to think of it that way with Cassidy.

What would she say if he asked her to stay on in Arrantino? If he told her he wanted to continue seeing her? It wasn't that much of a stretch. He could set her up in an apartment not unlike this one. He could get her a local job so that she was free to see him after work and on weekends.

But would she go for that?

And did he really want it? The fact that he was even considering doing all that to keep a woman in his life seemed crazy. But the alternative was that she fly back to New York, probably as early as tomorrow, and while he might not be one hundred percent sure about what he *did* want, he knew what he *didn't* want and that was for her to leave.

He liked waking up with her lying in bed beside him and he wasn't ready to say goodbye to that. And he knew she liked being with him this way. It was in every soft smile that she gave him, every tender touch.

He blew out a breath and contemplated the unpainted beams that crisscrossed the ceiling.

Unused to wanting something more with a woman than a good time, he found himself once again in the unusual position of not knowing how to proceed.

Cassidy stirred beside him, rubbing her calf along his leg, and he immediately thought about one way he could proceed—and a much less complicated one at that.

Shelving his vacillating thoughts with a much more pleasurable objective, he was about to roll her onto her back and press her into the mattress when he heard the first thump on his cousin's door.

Frowning, he didn't move just in case he'd been wrong when three extra-loud thumps followed.

Gently untangling himself from Cassidy, he murmured for her to remain asleep and rolled to his feet.

Given that he hadn't received much sleep the night before, his body wasn't impressed with being dragged out of bed as dawn touched the horizon and he padded grumpily downstairs to the front door.

'Your Majesty. It's Lukas.'

His head of his security?

Opening the door, Logan took in his grim demeanour. 'Your mother sent me.'

Instantly on high alert, Logan barely showed a flicker of emotion. 'Is she okay?'

'The Queen is fine, sir. But there's been a stir. In the news.'

A sense of dread even worse than when Leo had called washed over Logan. 'What kind of a stir?'

'The press have certain information.' He could tell his head of security was trying to be diplomatic and Logan strode over to the kitchen and switched on his phone.

A million messages pinged into the receiver, but he bypassed those and pulled up an international news site. A picture of Cassidy and himself at the look-out yesterday, his arms caging her in, her face turned sweetly up to his, was the first image that greeted him. The next ones were much more revealing.

'Logan, what is it?'

He heard Cassidy pad up behind him, leaning in to get a look over his shoulder before he could stop her. She gasped and he turned to find her fingers covering her mouth.

He glanced over her head at Lukas. 'How bad is it?' He knew Lukas would have already fully apprised himself of what had happened. 'And don't pull any punches.'

'A journalist, Todd Greene, has published an exposé on your relationship with Miss Ryan. He's included information on her family and interviews from her home town.'

Logan took one look at Cassidy's stricken face and frowned. 'This photo was taken yesterday. How can that be possible?'

'From what our intelligence agency has been able to ascertain, Greene had a local source. Someone who worked at the museum and was at the opening you attended last week talked about seeing the two of you together. It seems that Greene sniffed out the story and has been lying in wait to get photographic confirmation ever since.'

And Logan had given it to him.

He felt the rise of bloodlust in his veins and wasn't sure how he managed to not put his fist through a wall.

He glanced over to find Cassidy on her phone, her face chalk white.

Doing what he did best, Logan went into damage control. 'Cassidy?'

He had to say her name twice more before she registered that he was talking to her. He gripped her shoulders in his hands. 'Don't read any more. I'm going to fix this.'

'How?' her lower lip trembled and she staunchly bit down on it. 'You can't fix it. It's all true. Oh, God, he has those photos of me.' She hid her face in shame and Logan glanced at her screen to see an artless photo of a girl in cotton underwear that had clearly been taken years earlier.

'I sent it to a boy in the hope that he would like me. I never thought you would find out. I never thought *anyone* would find out. He promised that he and his friends had deleted the images…'

'God dammit,' Logan swore fiercely in the face of her open vulnerability. It was his fault that everyone knew about her past because anyone who came into his life was put under the microscope. 'You should have told me about this before now. I would have—'

What? Wrung the guy's neck along with that of every other person who had ever hurt his woman?

He ground his teeth, furious that someone would invade her privacy. Only just coming to understand how much he thought of Cassidy as his. Unable to process that right now, he turned his attention to what he needed to do next. 'Forget the photo. I'll fix it.'

She shook her head, barely listening to him. 'I need to call Peta.'

'It's the middle of the night in New York. Don't call yet.'

'Oh, no, the twins…' Her eyes scanned her phone. 'That bastard even interviewed their lowlife father!'

Wondering if she was about to be sick, Logan gave her a shake. 'I'll fix it.'

'You can't fix it.'

'I can. And I will.'

Oh, God, he was furious with her—and who could blame him after seeing *that* photo flashed all over the media with the caption *The King's New Sleaze*?

Bile rose in her throat. This was awful. Horrible. The worst possible thing that could have happened to either of them. And yet she couldn't blame Logan for being angry because he had probably thought that her past was as pristine as the women on his mother's marriage list. A list she knew she'd never make in a hundred years.

'What are you going to say about the two of us?' she asked hoarsely. 'Because I don't think *no comment* will cut it.'

'I'm going to close it down before it grows any more legs. You need to stay put and not get involved.'

Cassidy's stomach dropped into her toes. She supposed closing down whatever this was between them was the most obvious solution, and why wouldn't he take that route? She would have been leaving soon anyway. And probably the sooner the better because while she hadn't meant this to happen, her tarnished history had put Logan's kingship in jeopardy. And he was furious about it. Which she completely understood. He'd come to Arrantino on the back of one scandal—not to get involved in another.

And while logically she knew that it wasn't all her fault she couldn't bear being the reason someone was publicly slated. Just as she had been.

Dismayed, the threat of tears backed up in her throat, and she stared at the floor. 'I need to get home. I need to be with my family.'

'You need to stay here and trust me.'

'No.' She shook her head, everything inside her going ice cold. The last thing she needed to do was stay here and make it worse. She'd acted rashly by sleeping with him and now she'd face the consequences.

She crossed her arms over her chest. She'd indulged in a silly affair, *'put herself out there'*, and brought public shame on herself and her family again. And on Logan. 'I'm not waiting around for you to do anything. I want to go home. Now.'

'You're overreacting.'

'I'm *overreacting*?' She stared at him. 'My family name has been dragged through the mud for the world to see, you're being compared to your father, Leo's relationship is back in the news and you think I'm *overreacting*?'

'I know how bad this is,' he growled, dragging a hand through his hair. 'That's why I have to go. I have to fix it.'

'I knew this was a bad idea.' Her voice was a thread above a whisper, but he heard it.

'What was a bad idea?'

'Us.' She glanced around his cousin's apartment at the still full wine glasses on the bench, the uncorked bottle. She felt like soiled goods all over again. 'This.'

She had known it would be a mistake and she'd done it anyway so she had no one else to blame but herself.

Cassidy shook her head. What they had was a first-class mess. 'It doesn't matter now. Go.' She waved her hand in the air. 'I know you're desperate to get this under control.'

'I am. I will. Then we'll talk about what happens next.'

As far as Cassidy was concerned, she already knew what happened next.

'Your Majesty, I'm sorry to interrupt but—' Lukas stepped back into the room, his eyes on Logan '—Her Majesty is on the line.'

'Fine.' Taking a deep breath, Logan turned back to Cassidy.

Unable to stop herself, Cassidy reached out and pushed a lock of his hair back from his forehead.

'Wait for me.'

She shook her head. 'This isn't my home.'

Tension was stamped all over his handsome face. 'Lukas, I want you to personally take Miss Ryan back to the palace and make sure she's secure. Do not let anyone see her enter. I don't want to fan any more flames about this until I have it under control.'

Cassidy swallowed heavily. Of course he would be ashamed for anyone to keep associating them together when he had to correct this latest disaster. Her father had felt the same way when he'd returned home from work, asking if it was true that she had sent revealing photos to a boy at school. Having tried to weather the storm of her mother's desertion and Peta becoming a teenage mother, her mistake had been the straw that had finally broken the camel's back. And it only made her more resolved about her next move.

'Your Majesty.' A secret service agent in a black suit stopped beside him. 'The helicopter is ready when you are.'

Logan nodded, his eyes never leaving her.

Close to tears, Cassidy sniffed, her hungry gaze sweeping his face one last time, committing every one of his beautiful features to memory.

'Go,' she whispered. Go, before the hot tears scalding her eyes leaked out and revealed what she had only, in this awful moment, come to fully understand. That she did love him. Completely, and against all common sense.

She also knew that he needed to go into damage control for his family. That he would do his best to stifle this latest scandal and protect them. And she would do the same for him, and for her family.

She'd go home.

Logan paced his office, his shoulders tight, the muscles in his back aching. This had taken hours to pull together. Hours to ensure that every international outlet had agreed to pull the stories about Cassidy and her family in exchange for a bigger story.

Once that was done he'd put the world on notice.

Okay, his methods hadn't been entirely conventional, but neither was Todd Greene's revolting exposé.

But now he was drained and exhausted. He didn't think he'd fought for anything harder, or longer, than he had to ensure that Cassidy's decision to sleep with him did not completely destroy her reputation, or that of her family. He knew how important that would be to her. He knew how upsetting if he failed.

But finally it was done. His team had pulled off a miracle—for the most part.

The only tiny element of doubt in the whole thing was how Cassidy would react to the method he had used to close everything down. How she would react when he told her, and whether he could convince her that he'd done the right thing.

He'd never been this uncertain of anything in his life and he hated the voice in his head that said he'd overstepped. That this could backfire sensationally on him.

As his mother had angrily promised that it would. She didn't agree with the strategy he had come up with. In fact, she had turned around and walked out after she'd heard it, telling him that he was just like his father.

That had hurt.

But he hadn't let it sway him. He *was* like his father in many ways, but he knew he'd never betray the woman he had given his heart to. He'd never betray his family by turning his back on them. That was where they differed entirely.

They also differed in that Logan faced his problems head on and made decisions quickly to rectify them. It was what he did best. He only hoped he had made the right one this time.

With a few members of his team finishing up, Logan called Margaux into his office. She had done an amazing job of pulling various source materials together and he'd likely offer her the position as his private secretary when everything had settled down. 'Margaux, it's two in the morning. You need to go home. And don't rush in tomorrow. In fact, I'm fine if you want the day off. But tell me, has Cassidy called the office?'

'No, sir. Not that I'm aware of.'

She hadn't called him on his cell phone either. She was probably asleep.

In his bed or hers?

'But Gerome did leave a message earlier to say that he had taken care of Miss Ryan's request.'

'Request?' A cold feeling of dread chased away the anticipation firing his blood, everything in him going still. 'What request?'

'Apparently Miss Ryan left the palace some hours ago.'

'Left the palace?'

'Yes, sir. She wanted to be taken to the airport, so Gerome arranged a car. Is there something wrong, sir?'

Given his plans, yes. 'You should have told me earlier.'

'I'm sorry, I only checked the message five minutes ago.'

Logan dismissed her and turned toward the window, staring out at the dark night sky. She'd left, after he'd specifically asked her to wait. It didn't make sense. Why would she have done that?

Apart from the obvious—to get home.

'This isn't my home.'

Logan's jaw clenched. Well, it damned well was going to be if he had any say in it.

'Your Majesty?' Jason, his head of PR, spoke quietly behind him. 'If Miss Ryan isn't here, do you want us to pull the—?'

'No.' Emotion churned through him. Emotion mixed with a good deal of anger that she hadn't trusted him enough to sort this. 'Leave everything in play.'

A grim smile twisted his mouth.

In his country they had a saying he'd long lived by: *Al hombre osado la fortuna le da la mano.*

Fortune favours the brave.

He certainly hoped that held true because he had a feeling he would need it now more than ever.

CHAPTER THIRTEEN

'I CAN'T BELIEVE IT. They're still outside.'

Cassidy buried her head under her pillow against the evening sun streaming in through her back window as well as against her sister's voice.

'You should probably close the blinds,' she croaked. 'I've heard the paparazzi have telephoto lenses and if they come over the back fence they'll get what's called the money shot.'

Peta glanced out the window, a frown marring her brow. 'They wouldn't dare. Dan would take them out at the knees. He's already nearly come to blows with several of them out the front.'

Cassidy didn't want to hear that. The last thing she wanted was for Dan to get into trouble because of her.

It was all because of her.

She'd arrived home on a red-eye flight from Arrantino and found Dan waiting to pick her up. It had been such a relief to see him that she'd promptly collapsed in his arms and cried her heart out. All during the flight home she hadn't let herself think about actually having left Logan but as soon as she'd arrived on home turf it had become real and tiredness and emotional overload had overwhelmed her.

Dan had ushered her into his jeep and gunned it for the house, covering her with his jacket as they'd pushed their way through the mob of journalists outside her tiny Brooklyn home. The only upside, Peta had said, was that a few of their neighbours were loving every minute of the notoriety, dressing up and parading around just to see themselves on camera. Causing a distraction.

And telling the press that neither she nor Peta had ever been 'any trouble'.

If only that made her feel better.

'You're going to have to get up. You haven't eaten in twelve hours.'

And she might not eat ever again. It seemed like a viable solution to fixing the hole in her heart. Not to mention her reputation. Within twenty-four hours she had quit her job, slept with her boss, and become internationally unemployable. Quite a feat really, but not something that would look good on any future job applications. 'I'll get up soon.'

Peta perched on the end of her bed. They'd talked a little the night before, and Cassidy had apologised profusely, but her sister was holding up better than she'd thought she would be.

'I don't believe you,' Peta said. 'The girls will start to know that this is more than jet-lag if you don't show your face because it's not like you not to be able to pull it together.'

'I know.' She never let anything get to her, or at least

to let it show that it got to her, but she had no super-powers left. She was like Superman without his cape, or Batman without his tool belt.

Of course she knew she'd be all right. She knew once the dust settled, life would return to normal and she'd be able to push her feelings for Logan to one side and move on. It's what she did best. But she could see by the look on her sister's face that she was going to have some trouble convincing her of that.

'Sorry.' She pushed to a sitting position and shoved her tangled hair out of her face, grabbing her glasses from her nightstand to put them on before picking up her phone.

'No you don't.' Peta grabbed her cell from her. 'You've done enough Internet searches for the time being. It will only depress you.'

Knowing her sister was right, she subsided back against her pillow.

'I'm just so sorry you got dragged into it,' she said in a small voice.

'Don't sweat it.' Peta put on a brave face. 'And none of this guilt. I might not like having my life splashed all over the papers, but I've never lied to the twins about where they came from. They know their father abandoned them.'

'Yes, but now all their school friends will know. And your work.'

'We'll deal with it just the way we've always dealt with it. We'll start again.'

'But what about Dan?'

'He already knew everything, of course, but he said

that he'd stand by me. He said he'll go wherever the girls and I go.'

'Oh, Peta.' Cassidy had to fight back a wave of tears. 'I love you so much.'

Peta hugged her tight, stroking her hair. 'Half the reason this has been such a big deal is because of my wild teenage years. Seriously, you have to stop blaming yourself for everything that goes wrong.'

'You weren't responsible for that awful photo of me everyone is laughing at.'

'You were only eighteen, and a little too trusting at the time. And you could have been wearing a bikini. Really, Cass. No one will care in a day or two. Maybe a month.'

Cassidy tried to smile. She knew someone who would care. Logan.

'You'll see I'm right,' Peta said.

Cassidy tried to smile. 'I hope so.'

'The only question is what you do with yourself once that happens.'

'Move to Siberia.'

Peta laughed, wiping away a tear that had leaked out of Cassidy's eye without permission.

'I thought I'd cried out every tear in my body last night.'

'Unfortunately we produce more.'

Peta touched her forehead to Cassidy's. 'You're in love with him, aren't you?'

All the night before Cassidy had denied having any feelings for Logan, but she didn't know why she'd bothered. This was her sister, after all. 'Yes,' she said simply. 'Silly of me, isn't it?'

'I think you've always been a little in love with him,' Peta said softly. 'You never let a single person criticise him in your presence. It was as if the man really did walk on water.'

Hearing that only made her feel more miserable. 'Which means you were right to be worried. Something happened and it was my heart that was broken after all.'

'Maybe his is too. Maybe he loves you back.'

Cassidy sniffed and wiped her nose with a tissue. 'No. Desire isn't the same as love and that's all he feels for me.'

'Maybe you're wrong, maybe—'

A knock on the door startled them both.

'Sorry to intrude, ladies.' Dan poked his head around the door. 'But the twins just pulled this up on the Internet. It's an official palace statement. And apparently you can't find a mention of Peta or the girls on any of the main news sites. And believe me, the twins have searched every site known to man.'

Cassidy's heart beat out a slow, sad tattoo inside her chest. So Logan had closed it all down. She was glad. She only hoped the fallout on his side was somewhat mitigated by the lack of information out there now.

Peta took the laptop Dan held out to her and started to read, a strange smile curving her lips.

Cassidy gave her a quizzical look. 'What does it say?'

'It's a private statement from the King, explaining that his relationship with you is new and deeply private.

He's asked that the media respect your personal space and said he will prosecute any individual or group harassing his fiancée. It then says—'

'Fiancée?' Cassidy frowned. 'Are you sure you read that right?'

'I do know how to read.'

Cassidy held out her hand. 'Let me see that.'

She scanned the article, noting the official Arrantino seal and Logan's scrawling signature at the bottom of the letter. Then her eyes went back to the word *fiancée*.

'It must be a misprint,' she murmured. 'He must have meant assistant, or ex-assistant. He's probably furious with the error.'

Both Peta and Dan stared at her.

'Is it possible he thinks you're his fiancée?' Dan asked carefully.

'No.' Cassidy thought back to their last interaction. His anger with her and his intention to close everything down. 'No.' She shook her head. 'The concept is ludicrous.'

'Aunty Cassidy?' One of the twins poked her head around the corner of the door. 'Since you're awake we wondered if you wanted a cup of tea.'

Cassidy swiped at the tears on her face and gave her niece a hesitant smile. 'Thanks, April. That would be lovely.'

'And there's a man at the front door who wants to see you.' Amber nudged her twin out of the way. 'He looks sort of like the King of Arrantino, only way hotter.'

Cassidy felt goose bumps run up her arm, but immediately discounted that it was Logan.

'It's probably a hateful reporter,' Peta bit out.' I hope you didn't let him in.'

'No. He's waiting on the doorstep.'

'I'll handle it,' Cassidy decided, pushing out of bed and throwing a ratty old sweater over her singlet top and boxer shorts. She was tired of being the victim in this scenario. She'd said she was taking charge of her life and so she would. Starting with the hateful press. 'They need to understand that there's no story here and there never will be.'

Marching through their shambolic living room, she wrenched open the door. 'You have some nerve. Do you—?' The words instantly died on her lips as Logan turned back from scanning her street.

His blue eyes, surely brighter than they'd ever been before, grimly took her in from her awful bedhead right down to her bare toes.

Cassidy swallowed, wondering if she was dreaming.

Logan scowled. 'You didn't wait.'

She was so stunned to find him on her stoop she nearly fell sideways as he swept passed her and into her living room. Cassidy followed, finally managing to unstick her tongue from the roof of her mouth. 'What?'

Logan eyed her coolly. 'You said you'd wait.'

'Cassidy…' Peta's tentative voice came from the kitchen doorway, and trailed away as she recognised Logan standing like a conquering warlord in the middle of their tiny living room. Wearing a dark suit, and with legs braced wide apart, he looked magnificent.

'Your Majesty.'

Her sister dropped into a wonky curtsy, which made the twins, who were stood just out of sight, giggle.

'You must be Peta,' Logan said, managing to soften his features when he looked at her stunning sister. 'It's an honour to finally meet you. Please accept my heart-felt apologies for what the press has printed about you. I've done everything in my power to ensure that you, and all of your family members, will not be bothered again.'

'Thank you.'

Peta looked like she was about to apologise to Logan in return when Cassidy gave her a look.

'I'll just give you two a minute,' she said, backing out of the doorway and closing it behind her.

Reminded of just how Logan had tried to solve the problem, Cassidy frowned. 'I'm not sure you solved anything. In fact, you've no doubt made things worse.'

Logan turned the intensity of his gaze on her, which made her horribly aware of exactly what she must look like.

'You will not be bothered by the press any more, because I'm assigning bodyguards to all of you.'

'Bodyguards?'

'Yes.' He let out a breath. 'It won't be for ever. Just until the press understand the full consequences of hounding your family for information.'

'Okay, well, that's very nice of you, but not really necessary. When everyone realises that there's no story to write about, they'll disappear. Which would prob-ably happen a lot quicker if you hadn't actually shown up here today. The paparazzi must have gone crazy when you drove up the street.'

'My men cleared them out first. Although there is no doubt they will go crazy when they learn I'm here.'

'If you leave quickly enough, they won't.' Suddenly she realised that he *was* here and she had no idea *why*—unless it was just to apologise in person. 'Why are you here? It's nice of you to apologise to my sister in person, but a phone call would have worked just as well.'

'Not from my perspective.'

'Well...' Starting to feel nervous now that the adrenaline rush of having him in her home had worn off, Cassidy fidgeted with her shirt. 'You've said your piece so you can go.'

'I haven't said anything.' He gave her a hunted look and ran his hand through his hair. 'I need you to come back to Arrantino.'

'Why? If you're looking for a replacement, Margaux will be perfect. She knows everything.'

'I know. She might even eclipse you in some areas.'

Cassidy force a smile, trying not to let him see how much that hurt. 'Great. Excellent.'

She moved to straighten the twins' homework, which had been left haphazardly on the coffee table. Anything other than having him see how upset she was.

'The problem is,' Logan said softly coming up behind her, 'she's not you.'

Swallowing heavily, Cassidy straightened and turned to face him. 'That's nice, I suppose, but I can't come back to work for you. Is that why you're here? Because I thought—'

Logan clasped the tops of her arms, staying her words. 'That's not why I'm here. I don't want you to work for me. Did you not read the notice I put out at all?'

His eyes met hers, the usual arrogant sparkle in them missing. Cassidy swallowed heavily. 'Of course I read it. And I suggest you fix the typo pretty quickly if you haven't already.'

'It wasn't a typo.'

'You referred to me as your fiancée—ah!' Cassidy nodded, finally catching on. 'Clever.'

Logan frowned. 'What's clever?'

'Your strategy.' She nodded, wishing he'd used the phone instead of coming in person because she was struggling not to wind her arms around his waist and lean into him. She had thought that with time she'd get over never seeing him again but with him here now, larger than life, she knew that had been a fool's dream. 'Rather than deny that we had a fling, you're trying to make it look more serious so that the scandal factor is removed. But, honestly, with my history I wouldn't have gone with that, not to mention that your mother—'

'Cassidy.' He gave her a little shake. 'Be quiet.'

She blinked up at him, not sure if she should be offended or not.

'Sometimes you talk too much. The notice isn't a strategy. It's a plan. A plan you would have known about before the statement was released had you done what I asked and stayed at the palace.'

'A plan?' Her brow furrowed, her brain sluggishly

stuck on how good it felt to have him touching her. 'I don't think—'

'*Dios mio!*' His hands lifted to her face as he brought her body up against his. 'How I convinced myself for two years that I didn't want you I don't know.'

Instant desire slammed through her when he kissed her, her hands gripping his shoulders as she held onto him.

'Logan…' She was panting as she pulled back from him. 'You can't kiss me any more. It feels too good and I—' She shook herself out of his arms, shocked at how close she had come to revealing how she felt about him. The words *I love you* had been about to tumble from her lips.

'*Mi precioso amor*, look at me.'

Cassidy shook her head, resisting the hand beneath her chin as he tried to get her to look up at him.

'Don't hide from me,' he rasped. 'I don't ever want you to hide from me because I don't ever want to hide from you.'

Confused, she risked a glance up at him. The look in his eyes made her breath catch. 'You don't have to hide from me.'

'Good.' His hand stroked her hair back from her face. 'Because I love you and I want you to come back to Arrantino with me, as my Princess, not my EA.'

Cassidy blinked up at him, her brain still on a go-slow. 'You love me?'

His eyes scanned her face, his thumb tracing over her lips. 'So much I feel like it wants to burst from me.'

'But you don't do love. You said—'

'I've said a lot of things in my life that turn out not to be true. Love always seemed like a burden that was best avoided and I arrogantly assumed that I had control over how I felt. But I don't…' The emotion in his eyes was spellbinding. 'What I feel for you is beyond logic and control. It's like a part of me is missing when you're not beside me.' His smile turned soft. 'You make me smile even when you're not there.'

Cassidy felt tears well up in her eyes, spilling down her cheeks. 'Logan, I…' Clumsily she reached up and pulled his head down to hers, half laughing and half crying as she kissed him. 'Do you mean it?' she whispered. 'Do you really mean it?'

'You doubt me?'

'No.' She shook her head, a glorious laugh leaving her throat at his affronted look. 'I don't doubt you. I love you back.'

Her arms tightened around his neck as he lifted her off the floor and her legs wound around his waist. 'I love you so much I can't stop crying. But you know that I'm not princess material. That I'm not suitable. That photo—'

Logan made a dismissive sound. 'That photo is nothing.'

'I'm sure your mother doesn't think so. If she knew you were here—'

'She knows. And she will come round as soon as she gets to know you and realises that you're the most suitable woman in the world for me. You and no one else, *mi amor. Eres todo para mi.*'

'What does that mean?'

'You are everything to me.'

'Oh, Logan, I feel like I'm dreaming.'

His brow rose with mocking humour. 'And I'm not even half-naked.'

'Do not laugh about that,' she admonished. 'I felt so embarrassed to walk in on you half-dressed…not to mention totally aroused! I think it changed everything for me.'

'That's only fair because you have changed everything for me. You have made me a better person. A less cynical person, although I'm sure I'm not completely reformed.'

'I don't want to reform you. I just want to be with you.'

'Even though your life will never be your own again?' His expression turned serious. 'Because the life of a monarch is not for everyone.'

'I know that.' She stroked the rough stubble on his jaw. 'I'm not afraid of hard work and as challenging as it might be, as long as you're beside me I know that everything will be okay.'

'Then be with me, Cassidy.' His hand spanned her face. 'As my partner in life, as my Princess, as my wife.'

Bursting with the kind of happiness she had never expected to find, least of all with a man, Cassidy smiled giddily. 'Your wife?' She tightened her legs around him and heard him groan.

'Yes, it's the only role I'm willing to allow you to have in my life.'

Not waiting to hear her response, Logan kissed her with all the patience of a man hanging on by a thread.

'Aunty Cass—oops!'

'Oh, my stars, I told you two not to go in there,' Peta hissed at whichever twin had just opened the door.

'I need my homework. I didn't know they'd be fooling around like you and Dan do.'

When her sister squeaked in dismay Cassidy half groaned and half laughed. 'This is my family,' she said. 'Warts and all.'

Logan released her enough to let her feet slide to the floor. 'Your family is my family now, *mi amor*. They're perfect. Just like you.'

Cassidy didn't think it was possible to fall any harder for the man holding her so strongly in his arms, but she did then.

EPILOGUE

THE DAY OF the wedding dawned bright and blue. The vintage car had just dropped Cassidy at the entrance to the gothic cathedral in the centre of Trinia and the streets were lined with people waving banners and calling her name.

Cassidy had to blink back tears as she waved at everyone in return, her throat thick with emotion at the outpouring of support for her after the harrowing media scandal two months earlier.

Behind her Peta fanned out the train of her wedding dress, while the twins straightened her long veil.

'You look awesome, Aunty Cassidy,' April murmured, her wide smile full of joy, her hair fashioned in tiny plaits interspersed with white flowers.

'Like a real-life princess,' Amber agreed.

'You do,' Peta agreed, coming to stand in front of her, her soft lilac bridesmaid's gown the same shade as the twins'. 'You couldn't look more perfect, which is a surprise considering that your groom rushed the wedding.'

Cassidy grinned from behind her veil. Logan had

told her in no uncertain terms that he didn't want to wait to make their relationship official and that he considered two months a lifetime to make her his.

Secretly she'd agreed, but she had wanted to make sure that his mother was completely on board with everything before the wedding went ahead. Family had always been the most important thing for Cassidy, as it was for Logan, and she'd done everything that she could, followed every royal protocol, to prove that she was worthy of him.

That had paid off this morning when his mother had stopped by her room with two footmen in her wake carrying a very old, very intricate chest. Inside was a diamond teardrop tiara that had taken Cassidy's breath away.

'This was my mother's tiara,' she said. 'And her mother's before her. Since I didn't manage to have a daughter, I would be honoured if you chose to wear it today.'

Cassidy had felt herself choke up as she'd lifted the spectacular piece from its velvet bed. 'It's I who am honoured,' she said, biting her lip to stop the tears from falling.

Logan's mother had shaken her head. 'None of that. You'll ruin your make-up.' She had patted Cassidy's arm. 'I knew my son was enamoured of you very early on, but I didn't think you would fit. I was wrong. And one should never be afraid to admit that. Especially when you make my son so happy.'

'He makes me happy too,' Cassidy had said.

'As it should be. And now I will leave you to prepare

for the day ahead. But perhaps one night in the near future you could take a stroll with me around my rose garden. I'd be very pleased to show it to you.'

Cassidy had coloured at that, fervently hoping that there were no cameras in the rose garden to reveal exactly what had happened the last time she had been there.

Now she stood at the bottom of the stone steps, staring up at the towering church spire, her stomach alive with butterflies.

Suddenly she wished that Logan was beside her because she couldn't help feeling intimidated by what she was about to enter into.

As if her sister sensed it, she touched her arm. 'Don't stumble now, Your Highness,' she warned impishly. 'You have every camera on the planet aimed at you.'

'Thanks for reminding me,' Cassidy complained, her fingers trembling as she lifted them to smooth down her veil in the light breeze.

'Seriously, Cass,' her sister began softly. 'I know the King makes you very happy and if anyone deserves it you do. You've helped me out more times than I care to remember and now it's my turn to return the favour.' She held her arm out for Cassidy to take. 'Lean on me if you need to.'

Cassidy had asked Peta to walk her down the aisle and now she was very happy that she had. 'Thank you.' She placed her hand on her sister's arm. 'I love you.'

She turned one last time to wave to the crowd, before straightening her spine and gazing up at the entrance to the church.

The twins preceded her, scattering rose petals as they slowly made their way through the wide doors and up the aisle. Cassidy followed, with Peta beside her, her eyes riveted to the tall, handsome man waiting for her. He looked solid and steady and full of love as she made her way to him.

Barely noticing anyone else in the packed pews, she smiled up at him as Peta took her hand and laid it over his.

Logan gave her a slow grin. 'You look incredible, *mi preciosa*, but for a minute I thought I was going to have to send out a search party.'

Cassidy felt her whole body relax at his teasing tone, her heart overflowing. 'Not a chance, my love,' she whispered back. 'I'm yours for ever.'

* * * * *

Lost in the magic of
Crowning His Unlikely Princess?
Discover more stories by Michelle Conder!

The Italian's Virgin Acquisition
Bound to Her Desert Captor
The Billionaire's Virgin Temptation
Their Royal Wedding Bargain

Available now

**WE HOPE YOU ENJOYED
THIS BOOK FROM**

H HARLEQUIN

PRESENTS

Escape to exotic locations where passion knows no bounds.

Welcome to the glamorous lives of royals and billionaires, where passion knows no bounds. Be swept into a world of luxury, wealth and exotic locations.

8 NEW BOOKS AVAILABLE EVERY MONTH!

#3821 EXPECTING HIS BILLION-DOLLAR SCANDAL
Once Upon a Temptation
by Cathy Williams

Luca relished the fact his fling with Cordelia was driven by desire, not his wealth. Now their baby compels him to bring her into his sumptuous world. But to give Cordelia his heart? It's a price he can't pay...

#3822 TAMING THE BIG BAD BILLIONAIRE
Once Upon a Temptation
by Pippa Roscoe

Ella may be naive, but she's no pushover. Discovering Roman's lies, she can't pretend their passion-filled marriage never happened. He might see himself as a big bad wolf, but she knows he could be so much more...

#3823 THE FLAW IN HIS MARRIAGE PLAN
Once Upon a Temptation
by Tara Pammi

Family is *everything* to tycoon Vincenzo. The man who ruined his mother's life will pay. Vincenzo will wed his enemy's adopted daughter: Alessandra. The flaw in his plan? Their fiery attraction... and his need to protect her.

#3824 HIS INNOCENT'S PASSIONATE AWAKENING
Once Upon a Temptation
by Melanie Milburne

If there's a chance that marrying Artie will give his grandfather the will to live, Luca *must* do it. But he's determined to resist temptation. Until their scorching wedding kiss stirs the beauty to sensual new life!

YOU CAN FIND MORE INFORMATION ON UPCOMING HARLEQUIN TITLES, FREE EXCERPTS AND MORE AT HARLEQUIN.COM.

HPCNMRB0520

*The first time Scarlett sees Javiero after their
impassioned night together she's in labour with his
baby! But she won't accept empty vows—even if she
can't forget the pleasure they shared...and could
share again!*

*Read on for a sneak preview of Dani Collins's
next story for Harlequin Presents,*
Beauty and Her One-Night Baby.

Scarlett dropped her phone with a clatter.

She had been trying to call Kiara. Now she was taking in the
livid claw marks across Javiero's face, each pocked on either side
with the pinpricks of recently removed stitches. His dark brown
hair was longer than she'd ever seen it, perhaps gelled back from
the widow's peak at some point this morning, but it was mussed
and held a jagged part. He wore a black eye patch like a pirate, its
narrow band cutting a thin stripe across his temple and into his hair.

Maybe that's why his features looked as though they had been
set askew? His mouth was...not right. His upper lip was uneven
and the claw marks drew lines through his unkempt stubble all the
way down into his neck.

That was dangerously close to his jugular! Dear God, he had
nearly been killed.

She grasped at the edge of the sink, trying to stay on her feet
while she grew so light-headed at the thought of him dying that she
feared she would faint.

The ravages of his attack weren't what made him look so
forbidding and grim, though, she computed through her haze of

panic and anguish. No. The contemptuous glare in his one eye was for her. For this.

He flicked another outraged glance at her middle.

"I thought we were meeting in the boardroom." His voice sounded gravelly. Damaged as well? Or was that simply his true feelings toward her now? Deadly and completely devoid of any of the sensual admiration she'd sometimes heard in his tone.

Not that he'd ever been particularly warm toward her. He'd been aloof, indifferent, irritated, impatient, explosively passionate. Generous in the giving of pleasure. Of compliments. Then cold as she left. Disapproving. Malevolent.

Damningly silent.

And now he was…what? Ignoring that she was as big as a barn?

Her arteries were on fire with straight adrenaline, her heart pounding and her brain spinning with the way she was having to switch gears so fast. Her eyes were hot and her throat tight. Everything in her wanted to scream *help me*, but she'd been in enough tight spots to know this was all on her. Everything was always on her. She fought to keep her head and get through the next few minutes before she moved on to the next challenge.

Which was just a tiny trial called childbirth, but she would worry about that when she got to the hospital.

As the tingle of a fresh contraction began to pang in her lower back, she tightened her grip on the edge of the sink and gritted her teeth, trying to ignore the coming pain and hang on to what dregs of dignity she had left.

"I'm in labor," she said tightly. "It's yours."

Don't miss
Beauty and Her One-Night Baby.

Available June 2020 wherever
Harlequin Presents books and ebooks are sold.

Harlequin.com

Get 4 FREE REWARDS!